W9-BOB-736

Alameda County
LIBRARY
...Infinite possibilities

Opening Day Collection
2003
Purchased with funds
from the
City of Dublin

GIRL
GONE MISSING

Further Titles by J M Gregson

WATERMARKED
DEATH OF A NOBODY
ACCIDENT BY DESIGN
WHO SAW HIM DIE *
MISSING, PRESUMED DEAD *

available from Severn House

GIRL
GONE MISSING

J M Gregson

The first world edition published in Great Britain 1998 by
SEVERN HOUSE PUBLISHERS LTD of
9–15 High Street, Sutton, Surrey SM1 1DF.
First published in the USA 1998 by
SEVERN HOUSE PUBLISHERS INC., of
595 Madison Avenue, New York, NY 10022.

Copyright © 1998 by J M Gregson.

All rights reserved.
The moral right of the author has been asserted.

British Library Cataloguing in Publication Data

Gregson, J. M. (James Michael)
        Girl gone missing
        1.   Lambert, Superintendent (Fictitious character) – Fiction
        2.   Hook, Sergeant (Fictitious character) – Fiction
        3.   Police – England – Gloucestershire – Fiction
        4.   Detective and mystery stories
        1.   Title
        823.9'14 [F]

        ISBN 0-7278-5352-X

All situations in this publication are fictitious and
any resemblance to living persons is purely coincidental.

Typeset by Hewer Text Composition Services Limited,
Edinburgh, Scotland.
Printed and bound in Great Britain by
MPG Books Ltd, Bodmin, Cornwall.

Chapter One

MURDER takes place on the sidewalk. We have constant reminders of that. But as we reach the end of a violent century, violent death is not restricted to city centres. Killers are found in beautiful and remote places, as well as in ugly and crowded ones.

Not that the massive walls of Chepstow Castle, at the feet of which the corpse was found, are unfamiliar with death. They have stood on their cliff above the Wye, controlling the route into Wales, since William the Conqueror brought order to a disordered kingdom. They were the centre of vicious conflict in the Civil War in 1645, when the Wye which swirls below them ran red with English blood. But the castle is now a ruin, and Chepstow is a quiet town, far enough away from the points where the bridges carry the M4 motorway across the estuary of the Severn to be insulated from the noise and the bustle of the traffic which pours in and out of Wales.

There are no pavements visible beneath these mighty ramparts which have stood for almost a thousand years above the river. And the Wye, swirling here through the last of its picturesque bends to join the estuary of the Severn, is one of the most beautiful and unspoilt of Britain's rivers. Yet there can be death, even here. Violent and unnatural death.

The body had come down the river with the floods. It might have drifted ashore a few miles higher up at Tintern, where the angry brown waters had lapped against the stones of the ancient Cistercian abbey and washed three-piece suites from the villagers' cottages into the main street. But the macabre human detritus had swirled unseen past Tintern's soaring arches. On one of the great horseshoe bends where the swollen river ran beside Offa's Dyke, the body had become enmeshed with the twigs at the end of a great branch of gale-felled oak, and been carried thus to Chepstow.

The Wye Valley walk runs up the river from Chepstow, through some of the most beautiful waterside scenery the country can afford. But the young mother and her son were locals, happy to be enjoying a brisk afternoon stroll with the dog now that the October rains had finally relented. It was the dog, indeed, which discovered the river's grim cargo.

It was low tide, and the branch of oak with its sinister burden had come to rest on the mud flats opposite the high walls of the castle on the other bank of the Wye. In a few hours, branch and body would have been lifted softly but inexorably with the rising tide, the highest in Britain, moving up to fifty feet above the water's lowest level. And as the tide flowed swiftly outwards to the Severn estuary, the already badly damaged corpse would have been washed into the open sea, and perhaps lost for ever.

Instead, the labrador's curiosity took it ankle deep into the soft black mud, despite its owner's urgent shouts of recall. And when it saw what the branch held wrapped within its unseeing arms, the dog barked, excitedly, continuously, unstoppably.

The woman peered curiously at the source of the dog's excitement, then moved a pace or two further up the bank to get a better view of the dark bundle beneath the branches. At first she was not sure, swallowing back the sickness which rose to the back of her throat, telling herself that this thing could not be. Then she saw in the distance a grey-white hand, bloated, incomplete, damaged by the unseen creatures of the Wye. She screamed once, long and harsh, the sound ringing in her ears as though it came from a long way off. Then her maternal instincts took over and she gripped the nine-year-old hand firmly and protectively within her own.

She moved quickly back downstream, her face white and cold, the nausea she had felt heaving within her stilled by the urge to protect her son from this awful thing. The dog barked on for a moment, torn between the body and his owners, his head switching frantically between his find and his disappearing mistress. Then he left the mud and turned reluctantly back to the bank, afforded the branch and its burden a final volley of barks, and raced after the woman and child that represented food and shelter.

The woman found it difficult to steady her fingers in the phone-box. But 999 is an easy number to dial. Within minutes, the police machine was grinding into action. Within half an hour, the area was cordoned off and the police surgeon had confirmed that this was a human death.

Chapter Two

SUPERINTENDENT John Lambert was a patient man, in normal circumstances. And in these abnormal ones, he was determined to be at his most massively tolerant. Detective Sergeant Bert Hook was also a patient man. He was renowned for his composure in the Oldford CID section, even to the point where younger and more irreverent colleagues had been known to poke fun at his restraint in the face of provocation by the criminal fraternity. When it came to patience, DS Hook was a veritable Job among policemen. But this was golf. A game which brought a wholly unacceptable series of trials. Bert glared at his ball like a malevolent frog, his rubicund, village-bobby features swelling with an unaccustomed fury. "Bastard!" he yelled. "You bleeding, stupid, BASTARD thing!"

"That won't get the thing into the air," said Lambert with equanimity. "I know – I've tried it often enough."

"I know THAT!" snarled Hook, with unaccustomed emphasis. "But it might make me feel better." He did not take his eye off the ball. He felt an obscure certainty that if he did it would roll mischievously between his feet, would bring him crashing ignominiously to earth when he tried to move on. For it was already clear to him that this maddening white sphere had a will and impetus of its own and that its intentions towards him were malign.

"Just address the ball in your own time and swing slowly," said Lambert, massively calm.

Hook risked taking his eyes off the ball for an instant, so as to transfer the full fury of his gaze to his superior officer and mentor. When he swung his attention viciously back to the ball, it had not moved. It lay still among the twigs and the first yellow leaves of

4

autumn, where his last viciously topped effort had trundled it. "You can't even claim you got an impossible ball or a ridiculous decision at this bloody stupid game," he snarled morosely.

"That's the charm of golf," Lambert agreed, ignoring the glance of smouldering hatred the remark produced from his companion. "You're always really playing yourself, you see." His own ball was lying on the fairway, staring smugly up at him and asking to be hit, in Hook's view. Lambert selected a 7-iron, knowing privately that this was the club which carried for him the least chance of disaster, and dispatched his ball high and straight towards the green. It flew in a parabola which seemed impossibly high and graceful to his sergeant, pitched a few yards short, skirted a bunker and ran appealingly on to the emerald carpet of the green. Hook muttered something which sounded suspiciously like "clever bugger" and turned his attention miserably back to his own ball.

Bert aimed three more savage slashes at the uncooperative object, addressed it crudely as an intimate female organ to which it bore no obvious resemblance, picked it up, and strode to the next tee in a fury. John Lambert, schooled for nigh on thirty years in the worst excesses of police vocabulary, had never heard the gentle Bert use that word before, though he had little doubt that it had been addressed to obdurate batsmen in times of stress: Bert was a fast bowler of fearsome prowess, now retired from serious performance.

Hook was still red-faced and panting with frustration when Lambert arrived smiling at the tee. The Superintendent decided that it was not the moment to comment on the exhilarating nature of the day, with its warm south wind and white clouds flying against the crisp blue of the autumn sky. He had not seen Bert so ruffled since he had refereed a school football match and found ex-pupils chanting "Who's the bastard in the black?" from the safety of the beeches at the edge of the playing fields.

Yet golf is as unpredictable as it is exasperating. Salvation was at hand for the suffering Hook. The ninth hole at Oldford Golf course is a par three, only one hundred and forty-seven yards long. He took the 6-iron which Lambert counselled and teed his ball with an air of hopeless resignation, vowing for the tenth time that this would be his first and last visit to this place of torment.

Shutting his ears to his instructor's admonitions of rhythm and the straight left arm, he swung savagely and without hope at the tiny white target.

At first he did not see the ball. It was the gasp of astonishment from behind him which alerted him to the possibilities and raised his eyes towards the sky. The ball was up there, clear but impossibly high against the azure background. It stayed there for what seemed an impossibly long time, then pitched in the very centre of the green and stopped within a yard. An astonished smile spread very slowly over Bert's large face, until the visage was as round and delighted as his teenage face had been a quarter of a century earlier when he had bowled the great Gary Sobers in a charity match. "Bloody 'ell!" he said. Then, more quietly, and with the air of wonderment men produce in the face of great natural phenomena, he repeated softly, "BLOODY HELL!"

Lambert said, carefully keeping the surprise out of his voice, "There you are, I knew you could do it!" Almost as though he had produced the shot himself, Bert thought sourly.

The Superintendent addressed his ball carefully, feeling a sudden and unexpected pressure upon him. Perhaps he held his tall frame for a fraction too long over it. His shot was thinned; it reached scarcely half the height of Bert Hook's effort and curled inexorably right, into the deep bunker beside the green. There was a pause. Then Bert produced a carefully articulated "Hard luck, John". He found himself fighting hard against an inexplicable need to burst into uproarious laughter.

Lambert's lie in the sand was not a good one. He made three attempts to play it out: each one hit the steep face of the bunker in front of him and came to rest at his feet. When he picked his ball up and said, "Ah, bollocks to it!" Bert felt this was the first piece of golfing jargon which made complete sense to him. He turned his face towards the clubhouse and studied the clockface on the side of it determinedly, wishing he could stuff a handkerchief into his mouth to suppress the childish and inconvenient set of giggles which beset him.

They had switched off their radios on the course. Now, as they passed through the car park and made for the tenth tee in the

6

early evening, Lambert felt he should have a last check with the man they had left minding the shop at CID.

It was the tinny electronic tones of DI Christopher Rushton, high and thin beneath the yellowing leaves of the oaks, which drew them back from the schoolboy world of games to the savage reality of the world which was their everyday life. "We have a murder on our patch, Super," he said. "A girl. Eighteen, or thereabouts. Fished out of the Wye yesterday, at Chepstow. But it seems beyond doubt now that she's an Oldford girl."

It was obliging of the corpse to present itself at Chepstow. The town houses one of the seven laboratories run by the Home Office Forensic Science Service. The police 'death wagon' had only a two-mile journey to deposit the remains into the care of the forensic scientists.

On the morning after the news of the death had reached him, Lambert drove to the Chepstow laboratory. It was a bright October morning and his route ran along the A466 beside the sparkling Wye, through woods which were gathering the wistful glory of early autumn as the first yellow leaves appeared. He had been a policeman for too long to feel any guilt about enjoying the run on such a morning. He had already little doubt that this was a death which was sinister as well as tragic, but you grew used to death, to the need to distance yourself a little from even its most terrible manifestations. You had to survive and you had to remain objective.

You even had to feel a little excitement when a death became a murder, if you were a CID man. Violence kept you in business, provided you with the contests of wit and resource which were the reason why you followed such a strange occupation. So John Lambert enjoyed his drive. He even dawdled a little, as the sun rose high enough on his left to gild the trees and make the sheep of the ancient Forest of Dean skip as if this were spring rather than autumn. He had ample time to do so on this uncrowded route, for he had not arranged to meet the scientific officer who had conducted the post mortem until ten o'clock. It was five to ten when he turned his car into Usk Road and parked in the small area allotted to visitors beside the laboratory.

7

"Cliff Saunders," said the man from behind his office desk. He gave his visitor the curtest of nods and did not offer his hand. "I hope this won't take long." He was a short, spare man with a tightly trimmed beard; Lambert found himself wanting to ask if it wasn't inconvenient to him in his work. He was at least ten years younger than the superintendent, but curiously ill at ease, even though he was on his own ground. Not many people came into this place to discuss its findings, and Lambert sensed already that this was a man more at home with things than people, more at ease with the certainties of scientific investigation than the see-saw of conversational exchange.

As if to reinforce this impression, Saunders said aggressively, "I don't know what you expect to gain by talking to me. Everything I have to say will be contained in my official report. Your inspector has already had a verbal summary, and the full report is being typed as we speak. It will be with you first thing tomorrow."

"And I've no doubt it will be comprehensive," said Lambert evenly. "As comprehensive, that is, as a document can reasonably be, when it may eventually have to stand up to examination in a court of law. Cautiously comprehensive, as you might say."

"The report contains everything I have to say about this matter. The corpse was not in good condition, not even complete after all this time." The corners of his mouth turned downwards in a moue of distaste, as if he were a chef complaining that he had been asked to prepare a dish with inferior materials.

Lambert realised that there was no point in trying to explain his methods to this stiff creature, no point in trying to justify his need to get to grips with a case by gathering in the feelings as well as the findings of those involved, as this man now had been, however briefly and dispassionately. Intuition was sometimes a valuable quality for a detective, but Saunders would surely have no use for such an imprecise notion. No doubt he had turned eagerly from the uncertainties and untidiness of living humanity to the certainties of the dissecting table. A certain sort of mind demanded certainty above everything, and you could not carve up living bodies to provide definite answers to every question.

Lambert said only, "I find that it often helps me to talk to the man who has conducted an investigation into the causes of death. You'll have to take my word for that."

"I don't see how I can help you, that's all."

You wouldn't, of course. But then you're not used to being challenged, Lambert thought. He knew that he would gain nothing by offending this austere man. He said, "I'm aware that you have to be careful and precise in your findings; that they may be probed for weakness at some later date by some smart-alec lawyer." He saw from Saunders' face that he had struck a chord of recognition there, at any rate. "That is in itself a limitation. Sometimes it helps me if forensic men will go a little beyond the mere facts which are all they can safely put into an official report. Speculation may be dangerous in a legal context, but it can be helpful to policemen floundering after leads at the beginning of an investigation."

Saunders said woodenly, "I am not a doctor, Superintendent. I deal in facts. I am not at home with anything else."

Lambert had to resist the impulse to shout at the pompous twit that policemen also deal in facts, that he was here only because they wanted to establish the most important ones and proceed from there, that without facts they could never compile a case those cautious buggers from the Crown Prosecution Service would take up. Instead, he said doggedly, "Nevertheless, I think an exchange between us would be useful. Let's just go over the facts you have established for us and see if I have any questions, shall we?"

Saunders shrugged, then sighed petulantly. "If you think it will help. The cadaver had been in the water for a long time, you know. I should say ten to twelve weeks, though it's difficult to be certain."

His hand flashed comically to his mouth after these last words, and Lambert realised immediately that he had been more adventurous in speech than in writing: the summary DI Rushton had already communicated to him had spoken of eight to fourteen weeks. He did not underline the point that the forensic man was already being more precise in speech than in his report; the man had already realised that for himself. Saunders might be a prickly sod, but he was sharp and intelligent, and that was more important. "And the corpse has been in the Wye for the whole of that time?"

9

Saunders looked at him sharply. He had plainly not entertained the idea that the body might have been in other waters before it reached the river. It seemed unlikely, but it was possible, and a scientist must not disregard what was possible. The man found himself unexpectedly drawn towards the mystery that he thought he had already relinquished with his report, towards the puzzle which he now saw was just the first of many for this grizzled detective who sat so watchfully on the other side of his desk. "It's impossible to say for certain just where the body has been since death. It's certainly been in water for most of the period between the time of expiry and the hour when it was sighted in Chepstow. The deterioration and the damage from outside sources are what I would expect in a corpse immersed in a river like the Wye for ten to twelve weeks. The body was that of a young woman. Seventeen to twenty, I'd say. With a face too much damaged for normal identification, but a full set of teeth and recent dental treatment."

Lambert nodded. "We've already identified her from dental records. She was an eighteen-year-old schoolgirl from Oldford."

Despite himself, Saunders was suddenly and unexpectedly stricken with the pity of it, as the thing he had cut up turned suddenly from so much putrefying meat into a human creature, struck down at an age when she should have been full of aspiration and potential. He said dully, "You were quick. I only did the autopsy yesterday morning."

Lambert decided he might draw Saunders into the case if he offered a few of the facts the man seemed to find so reassuring. "There were twelve murders on our patch and the areas immediately surrounding it in the six weeks you gave us for the outside limits of this death. Nine of them were domestics; the other three all have a corpse present and correct. So we checked the missing persons register for our area. This girl was already registered as a MISPA – we scan the computer files automatically when we have a murder victim." Chris Rushton would be pleased to hear him singing the praises of the technology he often affected to despise, he thought with a grim smile.

Saunders digested the logic of these procedures, then nodded his satisfaction. "Well, it was murder, I should think. She didn't

10

die in the Wye, this one. She was dead when she went into the water."

"Alison Watts." She could have a name at least, even though such things were no longer of any concern to her. 'How do you think she died, Mr Saunders?"

A few minutes earlier, the man behind the desk would have bridled and said stiffly that his findings were in his report. Now he said, "Vagal inhibition. Asphyxiation or strangling, in layman's terms. But it's difficult to be absolutely precise as to how this came about. The neck has been too severely eaten away by the creatures of the river, you see. I showed the police liaison officer the problem when we were doing the PM. But I could get her out again if you'd like to—"

"No! No need for that. I understand the problem," said Lambert hastily. He found the man opposite him looking up in surprise at this unsuspected squeamishness in a senior officer.

"Well. I'm pretty sure from the damage to the internal organs of the throat that she was strangled. Probably with some sort of ligature. Rope or wire, in all probability; there isn't enough left to provide any detail of what sort of ligature, I'm afraid."

"So everything points to the fact that she's been in the river for a long time. But she couldn't have been dumped in the river near her home and taken this long to drift down to Chepstow, could she?"

"No. We've had plenty of rain in August and September this year. Even if a body got caught up in debris near the bank somewhere, it would have moved down to Chepstow within a week at most, I'd say. She was weighted down, Mr Lambert. There isn't much of her feet left, I'm afraid, but the injuries around her left ankle suggest that a rope or wire was tied round it – presumably with something heavy attached to the end of it."

The two of them were silent for a moment, picturing the incident two to three months ago when the body was slipped into the Wye, carefully weighted to guard against its discovery, probably somewhere near the girl's home, thirty miles upstream of where they sat. Then Cliff Saunders said quietly, "I imagine the rope detached itself when the foot was no longer there to retain it. Otherwise the poor kid might still be lying at the bottom of the

Wye." He was moved at last, this man who so spurned the use of the imagination, by his vision of the waste of this young life.

Lambert said slowly, "So she was killed somewhere away from the river – we don't know how far away – and dumped into the river at some point we may never find. Probably ten to twelve weeks ago." The facts were stark enough. He did not quote the statistic which showed that when murders were not solved within the first week, the chances of finding the culprit decreased sharply. No doubt a forensic biochemist was well aware of such facts.

Saunders said, "She wasn't a virgin. That's in my report, of course. But there was no chance of establishing whether this was a sex crime, I'm afraid. The flesh was much too far gone to ascertain whether there were any traces of bruising or scratching on the inner thighs, or anywhere else for that matter."

"No, I didn't expect there would be." And no semen or pubic hairs or clothes fibres from the man who had done this – if it was a man. The river had long removed such traces.

Saunders, appreciating now how his report provided many more questions than answers for the police, said, "The chemists are working on her clothes, but I don't hold out much hope for you there. Washed clean by the Wye, I'm sure." He had the air now of a man who wanted to help, who recognised the awful complexity of this death for the people who had to find out who was responsible for it. He weighed his thoughts for a moment, then said, almost reluctantly, "There's one other thing, which is only touched upon even in my report, because it's not a matter about which one can speak with certainty so long after death. There's not much of the genitalia left, but I'd say from the condition of the internal organs that this was a girl who was sexually active. Frequent intercourse, I should think. Whether with one partner or several, you'll no doubt find out in the course of your enquiries."

It had cost this constricted man quite a lot to move from the facts of his dissecting slab into such speculation, and both of them knew it. Lambert stood up. "I expect you have daughters yourself, as I have." Saunders nodded bleakly. "Thank you for your help. I don't suppose anything more will occur to you, but if you should think of something else which might be of help, please ring me."

12

The scientist nodded. "Where will you begin?"

"With the people who were with her last. With her family, to start with. And no doubt in due course with her sexual partner, or partners."

None of these, of course, might be the person who was with her last of all, the person who had abruptly stilled this young life and watched her weighted body sink into the depths of the Wye. Starting so long after the event, it might be that they would never discover that ruthless operator. It wasn't an investigation to look forward to.

And the victim was beginning to emerge now as a real person, not the cipher she had been when John Lambert had enjoyed the colours of the forest and the glint of the river on his way to Chepstow. The drive back to Oldford, shadowed now with this death and its consequences, would be altogether more sombre.

Chapter Three

IN the event, it was Bert Hook who got the job of breaking the news of the girl's death to her parents. He took a young WPC with him and went round to the house in the early evening.

Alison Watts had lived in a small modern house, privately owned, built in the middle eighties, when people were scrambling to acquire property, before the slump in prices which destroyed confidence and left buyers trapped in the negative equity of the following decade. These were the cheapest Oldford houses erected in that period; the builder had avoided all frills to keep his prices to a minimum, knowing that almost anything would sell to those who kept work and prospered as the numbers of unemployed rose steadily. Central heating meant no fireplaces, which in turn meant no chimneys and an unbroken roof skyline. It all added to the boxy uniformity of these neat, depressing terraces. Some of the small front gardens were still bright with the remains of summer bedding. But Number One, The Lawns, had a lawn that needed mowing and an uneven privet hedge that needed cutting. There were no flowers in its ragged borders.

The man who opened the blue front door of the end-of-terrace house had a two-day growth of beard. Bert would have liked to ask the young woman in uniform at his side whether she thought this represented fashion, laziness, or worse, because to an old-fashioned policeman it just looked untidy. Instead, he said, "Mr Watts? We spoke on the phone about this. It would be better if we came inside, I think."

The man stared at them for a moment, then turned and led the way into a lounge that was tidy apart from the single beer-can on top of the television set in the corner of the room. They had passed a vacuum cleaner in the hall; perhaps someone had been cleaning

14

the place in the twenty minutes since his phone call. Hook and his WPC sat demurely at opposite ends of the sofa and Bert said, "I assume that you are Robert Watts, the father of Alison."

"That's right. Well, stepfather really, I suppose, but I've always treated her as if she were my own daughter. I've been around since she was four or five, you see." The man was not at ease; he scratched his close-cropped hair, then let his index finger dwell experimentally for a moment on the tiny scab on his cheek, as if he wished he could prise it away and dispose of it.

But perhaps it was a blanket hostility towards the police, or even towards authority generally. To Bert Hook, studying him closely, Watts did not seem unduly worried or distressed by this visit. Four fifths of suspicious deaths took place within the family, so until they knew more about how Alison Watts had died every member of this particular one would be inspected for any suggestion of guilt, for any sign of the knowledge that could lead the police to a solution.

Hook's ears had been listening automatically for sounds of movement in other rooms since they had first set foot in the hall: police personnel of any rank did this instinctively in all kinds of situations, as much from an urge towards self-preservation as anything else. This small modern house, where the thin walls and floors would surely have given away any movement, seemed very empty. Hook said, "Is Mrs Watts around? It would really be much better if we could speak to the two of you together."

"No. Not at present, she isn't." It sounded abrupt, even aggressive. But perhaps he was just nervous, full of a sense of doom after their phone call. People usually anticipated bad news, even when they hoped desperately for the best.

WPC Hogan, anxious to have some part in this macabre cameo – she was so new that this was her first suspicious death – said, "Will she be back soon? It really would be much better for you if she heard this from us, you see, and—"

"Heard what?" There was no doubt of his aggression now. Bert had met the attitude many times over the years: suspicion of the police, a reluctance to cooperate which developed into truculence. This man wanted them out of the house as quickly as possible, as if they polluted the place with their very presence.

15

But Watts had lost his daughter, or stepdaughter. A girl whom he had probably loved, who had been the embodiment of his hopes for the future. Hook said, "When do you expect your wife to be back, Mr Watts? It really would be better if she could hear what we have to say at the same time as you."

"I don't know when she'll be back. Not today."

"I see. Where is she, Mr Watts?"

The man's face darkened. Hook was aware of the still but excited white features of Liz Hogan over her notebook. No doubt she was entertaining notions of Robert Watts as a mass murderer, who had disposed of his wife and God knew who else as well as his daughter: John Lambert always said that young police imaginations worked in full technicolour. And the gory slaughterhouse of the awful Fred West was within twenty miles of here, a perpetual reminder to the police officers in the area of the depths to which humanity could sink.

And for a moment Watts seemed as though he was about to further such fantasies. He sprang suddenly to his feet and turned away from them, staring unseeingly through the window to where a washing line arched towards its invisible hook. He wore light blue jeans, still stiff with newness, and a sweater which was rucked up at one side. His slip-on shoes were worn a little at the heels and badly scuffed at the toes, as if he had knelt on concrete in them and never rectified the damage. The watch he glanced at now looked as if it had cost a lot more than all of his clothes. He turned back to them and said, "The wife's away for a few days. I don't know where she is, nor when she'll be back. You'd best tell me about Alison, and I'll let Kate know about it in due course."

Hook didn't like it. He'd been prepared for grief, for hysterics, even for anger – people in the agony of grief sometimes needed someone to blame, and the police were conveniently at hand as the messengers of death. But the man clearly had a right to know: they couldn't withhold information. He said in his soft Gloucestershire tones, "You'd best sit down, Mr Watts. It's not good news we bring."

Watts came and sat down opposite them. He moved rather in slow motion, like a man walking carefully towards what was inevitable. It was almost as though he knew already, thought Hook. But then most people had premonitions of disaster, when their children went missing; Watts might be merely anticipating the worst, seeing the nightmares he had endured in the weeks since the girl's disappearance become reality before his eyes. Bert said, as evenly and officially as he could, "A body has been recovered from the Wye at Chepstow. It had been in the water for some time. About the same period as that which has elapsed since you reported Alison to us as a missing person. It seems—"

"It's Alison, isn't it? I knew it, all along. We tried to think it wasn't, but I knew it, from that first weekend when she disappeared." Until now he had been abrupt, even hostile. Now he spoke quietly, deliberately, like one in a trance.

Hook said, "I'm afraid there's no doubt, sir. You were kind enough to give us access to Alison's dental records when you registered her as a missing person, you see, and we've checked them. It's a reliable method of identification, in these circumstances."

Watts stared at him for a long moment, slowly re-focusing his attention upon the world around him. He said, "There wasn't much of her left, I suppose." Then he nodded slowly, his chin jutting out as it rose and fell, as if it were a hammer tapping the idea of the girl's death into his brain.

Hook said, "She wouldn't have been easy to identify by the normal methods, no. But fortunately there's no need for that, now. But we can't release her body for a funeral yet, I'm afraid. There'll have to be an inquest. And I'm sorry to tell you that the police will be telling the Coroner that they see the circumstances of her death as suspicious." He paused, waiting for a reaction. The official circumlocutions were the safest, but when people were smitten with grief they did not always understand them.

This man did. "You mean someone killed Alison."

"It seems like it. She didn't drown, you see. She was dead before she went into the river." Hook watched his man closely as he delivered the brutal facts. You had to assess how much people could take, when you brought news like this. But much more important, you had to watch for any tell-tale reactions which would connect a relative with a killing. This man did not seem very upset or very surprised by what they had to tell him.

But after a moment when he stared stony-faced at Hook, he buried his face in his hands. "She was a good girl," he said in a strangled voice between his fingers. When he dropped his hands, his face was still dry, but his features were twisted with emotion. "Spirited, yes. What adolescent girl doesn't give you a little trouble, cause a few shouting matches in the family? But we loved her, and she loved us."

WPC Hogan took her cue and made ready to record things in her still pristine notebook. "Then I'm sure you'll be as anxious as us to track down whoever did this awful thing, Mr Watts. We need to speak to all the people who were in close contact with Alison in the time before she died. For a start, can you tell me what was the last time you saw her yourself?"

"Yes. I saw her here at six-thirty on Friday the twenty-third of July." She must have shown her surprise at the immediate precision of his answer, for he added impatiently, "I've told your people all of this before. She went out on that Friday night and never came back."

Hook said, "Yes. It's on Alison's file as a missing person. But I'm afraid you must be prepared to go over the same ground again in the next few days, Mr Watts. Now that this has become a murder enquiry, different officers will be involved."

"More senior men, you mean." Watts did not disguise his contempt. "And I expect you'll give the case a higher profile, now it's murder. More kudos in it for you lot, I expect, bringing in a killer."

Hook didn't dispute it. It was all true, even if it wasn't the whole truth. He said, "There are many thousands of young people who go missing, Mr Watts. Most of them turn up safe and well, eventually. There simply aren't the resources to follow all of them up in detail. If they're over eighteen, we don't have the right to bring them back to their parents, unless they want to come."

"Well, this one didn't turn up, did she? So now you've got a murder on your hands." He sounded at that moment as if that was a satisfactory outcome to him, if it embarrassed the police.

Hook said evenly, "Alison was an only child, wasn't she, Mr Watts? We shall be talking to her mother, of course, as soon as we find where she is." He let the words hang in the air for a moment, but Watts did not react. "In the meantime, we need to know the names of people who were close to her. Friends, relatives, anyone who—"

"Go to the school. Ask there. I hardly saw her during the week, did I? I wouldn't know who her friends were, what she was doing. She only lived here, didn't she? Only came to me when she wanted money."

It was bitter, disillusioned, a contradiction of the tenderness he had professed so recently for the girl. But it was not so different from what they heard from many a parent. And Alison Watts was not available to put her side of the story. Murder was the only crime where you had to build up a picture of the central figure wholly through the viewpoints of other people, all with their own reasons to like or dislike that figure.

"Alison was at Oldford Comprehensive, wasn't she? In the sixth form."

"If you know that, why come wasting your time here? Talk to her friends there. Talk to her bloody teachers, for God's sake!"

Hook thought there might be something interesting in that last, vehement emphasis. But this wasn't the time or the place to follow it up, with a man who was becoming increasingly hostile to them. He stood up, looking round the tidy, soulless room. There was no trace of a photograph of the dead girl; in his experience, that was unusual, with an only daughter. He said, "We shall visit the school in due course, Mr Watts. If your wife returns, please ask her to get in touch with us immediately. Thank you for your help." He was on his way out before Watts could detect any irony in the remark.

At the other end of the terrace of houses, a woman stood in her small front garden. She was cutting a bunch of Michaelmas daisies, but the way she looked at the police car as they got into it suggested to Hook, who was something of an expert in such things, that she had been waiting for them to emerge from the Watts' house. He turned the corner, so that he was out of sight from any of Robert Watts' windows, and drew the car quietly to the kerb. Sure enough, the woman bustled after them and stepped conspiratorially over the low garden wall as he lowered the window of the car.

19

"Been talkin' to 'im, 'ave you? Not before time, if you ask me! Tell you where Kate was, did he? Where 'e'd put 'er, more like."

This woman couldn't yet know about the death of Alison Watts. She was talking about something else, something almost as dramatic, in her view. But she might know where the girl's mother was. Hook said, "No, Mr Watts didn't tell us where his wife was. He said he didn't know where she'd gone."

"Didn't know? Wasn't telling, more like." The woman sniffed truculently, clutching the stems of her Michaelmas daisies more tightly; the blue flower-heads trembled dramatically, seeming to reflect her indignation.

"If you know where Mrs Watts is, you should tell us. We need to get in touch with her urgently, you see."

The woman was about fifty and looked as if she led a drab life. She sensed a drama in Hook's word 'urgently', one in which she might have a vicarious, peripheral role. Her eyes narrowed with the triumph of her knowledge. "She's in the refuge, isn't she, Katie Watts? The refuge for battered wives, where they take them in to protect them from their husbands!"

Chapter Four

THOMAS Murray was a modern educationist. Oldford Comprehensive was lucky to have him as its headmaster. The Governors
thought so. The Chief Education Officer thought so. In his more
expansive moments, when he saw the mistakes some other head
teachers made, even Tom Murray thought so.

Murray was shrewd as well as intelligent, a man who understood
the strengths and weaknesses of the state education system, and
made use of both of them. Most of the general public expected
teachers to be dedicated, a little unworldly in the rewards they
expected; Tom Murray was aware of that. The fact that the system
was supposed to be above and beyond petty considerations of
personal advancement only made it the more vulnerable to him.

Murray was not just a con man: his progress had necessitated
a much greater range of skills than that. He was a sound, efficient
teacher; he had demonstrated that in his early days. That did
not mean he was brilliant or original; Tom learned early in his
educational life that these were qualities which the hierarchy
distrusted, however much they might pay lip-service to them.
Soundness. Reliability. Those were the attibutes hard-pressed head
teachers looked for in their junior staff. So the young Tom Murray
had provided them: he quickly acquired a reputation not just for
being adequate in the classroom but adept in handling both parents
and those visiting public and educational dignitaries upon whom a
school's reputation depended. He became a Head of Department
in a large secondary school when he was twenty-nine.

Now it was necessary to look beyond the school itself to the
educational world at large. Murray took the *Times Educational
Supplement* and read the articles at the front of the weekly journal
as well as the lists of jobs at the back which preoccupied his

colleagues. He became an expert on educational ideas; more important, his shrewdness enabled him to spot which ones to support as educational fashions changed. He enthused over the child-centred approach to education of the 'seventies, and his progressive ideals carried him to a Deputy Headship at thirty-five.

He was diligent, efficient and hard-working. His head teacher, a man twenty years older than Tom, found him an able supporter to whom he could safely leave much of the public relations work which seemed to be increasingly important in education. And Tom saw how events were moving against the progressive ideals of the child-centred approach to education more quickly than most of his colleagues. He began first to question and then to deride what he now called the wishy-washy ideals of learning which was built round the needs of the individual child. "Progressive", the by-word of his early years in schools, now became an insult, and Tom learned to pronounce it with a curl of his wide, expressive lips. He devised a ringing call for a return to basics in education, to the old ideals of discipline and measured progress; it went down well at interviews. At forty-one, he was appointed Head Teacher of the Oldford Comprehensive School, one of the county's largest. He had reached his goal.

There were a few casualties of his progress, of course. That was inevitable. He had to give up most of his hobbies. But his marriage to the dutiful, supportive girl he had met in his last year at university survived. There were two children, but they did not have to attend his school, because he had taken the precaution of living some miles away from it, in a village out towards Cheltenham. His children were not in his own school's catchment area, so their teenage troubles could not be the subject of sniggering at his expense behind the staffroom door of his school. And if his marriage was not as exciting as others he heard and read about, well, there were ways of adding a little excitement to your private life, if you were well organised and discreet. Tom Murray was both.

On this bright October morning, Mr Murray shut himself away in the headmaster's office as soon as assembly was over, with orders that he was not to be disturbed. There was not much time to gather his thoughts. The police would be here in twenty minutes.

They had not said much on the phone. Just that it was about his missing sixth form girl, Alison Watts. But this time it was CID. A Detective Sergeant, who had made the call, and a Superintendent. Big stuff: that meant the news must be bad. Almost certainly the wretched girl was dead. Bad publicity for the school. But then they said there was no such thing as bad publicity, and that seemed to become more true with each passing year. At least the girl's death would keep Oldford Comprehensive in the public eye. The public reaction must be a sympathetic one, though, if anything useful was to come out of this business.

Tom took a pad out of the top drawer of his desk and began to rough out his statement for the press. "Alison was a lively, intelligent girl. One of the most popular girls in the school. She was a prefect and a much respected member of our school community, and she would certainly have gone on to gain a university place and do well there. Our hearts go out to her family at this tragic time." Perhaps he should describe her as a "young woman" rather than a girl; that would give it a bit more dignity, and emphasize the level of education within his school. But what he had scribbled would do for a start; he would polish the phrasing later, when he knew how much detail of the death the police were going to reveal. Eventually, he would add something about the necessity to put behind bars whoever had done this awful thing, but not yet. Ever since she had gone missing, he had let it be known privately that he thought a girl who behaved as Alison had done could come to no good. But he mustn't commit anything to paper about the manner of her death at this stage. Not until the police had said something official.

His secretary brought the policemen in. They were in plain clothes, of course. The Superintendent was tall and thin, with plentiful dark hair which was grizzled with silver and a long, lined face; he had grey, watchful eyes and the beginnings of a tall man's stoop. Even as he introduced himself as John Lambert and shook hands, he studied Murray. The head was conscious of being assessed, in this room where most people who

23

entered felt at a disadvantage with him; he found it unexpectedly disturbing.

Detective Sergeant Hook was altogether less threatening. With his ruddy, countryman's countenance and his ready smile, he seemed much more the kind of policeman who should be coming into schools and dealing with children. Tom Murray could see him in uniform, instructing much younger children about the safety code for pedestrians and cyclists. But he would go carefully with this Superintendent chap.

Lambert said, "It's bad news, I'm afraid. I expect you guessed that."

Tom had a strange feeling that the thoughts he had indulged before they came were being laid bare for the inspection of those cool grey eyes. "I feared the worst, yes. One always hopes against hope, of course, but—"

"Quite. The body of a young woman was retrieved from the Wye at Chepstow two days ago. We are now quite certain that it is that of Alison Watts."

Now that the moment of revelation had come, Tom Murray felt oddly unprepared for it. He was searching for the right reaction, when he should not have even needed to think about it. There was a pause that should not have been there before he said, "Oh dear. She was a girl with everything to look forward to. Was it – was it some sort of accident? I can't think that Alison would have done anything foolish, even with the traumas which seem to loom so large as we pass through adolescence—"

Lambert let his words peter out, when he had expected to be interrupted. It made them sound curiously hollow. Then the Superintendent said, "Miss Watts's death wasn't an accident, Mr Murray. And neither was it suicide. That's why we're here. The girl was murdered."

"But how can you be sure that . . . You said she was pulled out of the river. I naturally assumed that—" Again Lambert let him go on, studying him steadily as he spoke. And again Tom Murray felt that his words acquired an unreal, theatrical edge, as if he were speaking lines in a bad stage thriller.

"I didn't say that she drowned, though. Perhaps I should have made myself clearer. Alison Watts was dead before she ever went

24

into the Wye. The details will be revealed at the inquest, but I can tell you now that she was strangled. By person or persons unknown. It's our job to make them known. That's why we're here."

"Yes. Yes, I see. And of course we must do everything we can to help you, Superintendent. It's just rather a shock, you see, to find that one of our girls, who was with us for seven years, has been killed so brutally. It's – it's a little like losing one of the family, you see."

It was overstated, and Lambert let the overstatement hang in the air for a moment, in which its falsity seemed to grow. It was almost as though the words, conventional as they had seemed to Murray, were weighed and found wanting by this disconcerting visitor. Eventually he said, "We shall need your full cooperation, and that of your colleagues. We're starting a murder investigation late, far too late. Our initial enquiries suggest Miss Watts died eleven weeks ago."

"Just after the end of our summer term, then." With a reaction that had become instinctive over years of dealing with the local media, Murray began to distance the death from his school.

"Yes. We're assuming until we find anything to convince us otherwise that she died shortly after she disappeared. We shall need to talk to both her teachers and her friends in the school. We need to piece together a picture of the girl and her movements both in her last hours and in the weeks before her death."

"Yes, of course, I see that. I'm sure everyone here will be only too anxious to help resolve this terrible business."

Again he found his conventional sentiment was examined, when it was not strong enough to bear such scrutiny. Then there came an assault from where he had least expected it. The rubicund Sergeant Hook, notebook at the ready, said without warning, "When did you last see Miss Watts alive yourself, Mr Murray?"

Tom tried not to look ruffled that he should be asked the question. He had half-expected it when Alison first disappeared, but the uniformed men had scarcely spoken to him in July. He supposed that he should always have been prepared for it. But he found now that he was not. Not at the outset, and so abruptly. These men behaved as though directness was a habit and they expected directness and simplicity in his replies. He realised how much preliminary fencing, how much polite, irrelevant nonsense went on in this room, as he put visitors at their ease and they put off saying what they had really come about in the early stages of conversation. Without these habits, without this greasing of the wheels of exchange, he felt very exposed.

He said carefully, "It's a long time now since the end of our summer term. But I think I spoke to the first year sixth on the last Thursday – the term ended formally on the Friday. Gave them a little pep talk about the importance of what for most of them would be their final year in the school as they came up to their A levels and looked for entry into higher education – a very high proportion of our boys and girls go off to universities, you know." He dropped unthinkingly with this last phrase into the mode of address he used for local councillors.

Hook said, "And Alison Watts was there among that group. You're saying that that was the last time you saw her."

"If she was there, yes. I really can't recall at this distance of time whether a single girl among nine hundred in my school was present in a large group."

He allowed himself a flash of petulance as he felt on safer ground. He knew the way a school worked, and these intrusive men didn't. It was the area to assert himself. But it didn't have the effect he desired. Lambert said sharply, "Of course not, in normal circumstances. But these are scarcely normal. The girl was registered some time ago as a missing person, and enquiries have already been made in the school by other officers. I'm surprised you haven't already asked yourself when was the last occasion on which you saw the girl."

It was a direct challenge, which left Tom Murray feeling a little foolish. He said sullenly, "I have done that, of course. But this is a busy school, and I have had a thousand other problems in the weeks since the girl went missing and your uniformed men came in to ask us about where we thought she might have gone. Yes, I seem to recall now that Alison Watts was in the group I spoke to on that Thursday. That would indeed be the last time I spoke to her. And as I told the people who came here originally when she went missing, I didn't speak to her individually, and I didn't see her again after that meeting."

26

"Thank you," said Hook. He made a note in his round hand. "What were your impressions of Alison Watts? Was there anything unusual in her way of life? Anything which distinguished her from others in the group?"

"No." Tom wondered if his negative had come a little too promptly and insistently. "She was an intelligent, lively girl. A credit to herself and the school. I can't think of anyone who would have wished her any harm."

It sounded even in his own ears like a prepared, empty statement, and Hook treated it as such, not even bothering to record this reaction. He said, "We shall need to speak to those of your staff who were in daily contact with the deceased girl."

"Yes, of course. The best person for you to start with is Margaret Peplow. I'll get my secretary to take you across to see Mrs Peplow now. She's our Director of Sixth Form Studies."

Titles had got more grandiose since he was at school, thought Lambert. Well, schools didn't exist in vacuums: they were part of society; it was inevitable that they should reflect its small vanities, as well as its greater evils. He said, "Thank you for your help, Mr Murray. We shall disturb the life of the school as little as possible, but I must ask you to remember that this is a murder enquiry: it is our duty to do whatever is necessary to conclude it. Goodbye for the moment. We shall no doubt need to see you again in due course."

The words rang in Tom Murray's ears even after he heard his secretary taking them out of her room and into the corridor. They sounded to him almost like a threat.

He looked out of his window and watched his visitors moving swiftly across the wide quadrangle within the modern red-brick blocks of his school to the sixth form complex. He went over again in his mind what had passed between him and them. The content of it seemed straightforward enough, even if he had been thrown off balance by their manner. He could not see how they could possibly have spotted his concealments.

Chapter Five

MARGARET Peplow did not fit the conventional view of a schoolmarm. She was a slim, dark-haired woman of thirty-nine, with an unlined face and sparkling black eyes. The Head's secretary had informed her of their arrival, and she came out from her office to meet them. Hook noted a trim figure, a skirt which suggested the contours of her figure without stretching too explicitly over her rear, as she led them through a large, carpeted room which had easy chairs and a drinks machine and the notice 'Sixth Form Common Room' on the door.

"Bit different from my day!" said Lambert. He looked round appreciatively at the room and the decor, lest Mrs Peplow detected a personal note: she was indeed a considerable improvement on 'Chalky' Morton, who had taught a gawky John Lambert about *Hamlet* and Hardy and reeked of pipe tobacco and hair pomade. But he had better not say so. Their guide looked round the room and grinned. "Bit of a con trick, really, I suppose," she said with a grin. "We didn't get this until we started to lose our students to the further education college. They like to feel they're no longer schoolchildren when they've finished their GCSEs. And why shouldn't they? They're old enough to vote by the time they leave here. And a lot of them have part-time jobs at the weekends, however much we affect to disapprove of such things." She looked back at the large, empty room as she led them into her office. "It's not big enough, of course, when all the lads and lasses get together at lunch times, but they like it. You can almost hear the adolescent hormones rattling around in there at times."

"And Alison Watts was part of all that? No different from any other girl?"

"They're all different, Mr Lambert. Every kid is an individual.

28

Educational theory insists upon it." The dark eyes twinkled at them, when they had expected her to be conventionally cowed by this death. "When they become old enough to be called students, they insist upon it themselves. But yes, Alison Watts had the same urges as most girls in late adolescence. She was as interested in boys as most of her peers. Long before you reach her age, it's a status symbol to have a boyfriend, especially in a co-educational school. Alison had got beyond that stage: she was a young woman, old enough to vote. She'd missed a year out through a school change when she was much younger, so that she was a year older than most of her group. She knew she was pretty, that she had no difficulty in attracting boys. Even men, when she wanted them."

Lambert looked at her sharply. "Men? Presumably you have some reason for saying that, Mrs Peplow?"

"Not really. It was rather a silly thing to say. I was just emphasising that Miss Watts was a young woman, not a schoolgirl, I suppose. I have no doubt that she led quite a full life outside the school." But this composed, humorous woman had been disconcerted for an instant, as if conscious of her own indiscretion. It had been no more than a fleeting moment, and she had recovered herself just as quickly.

Lambert said, "We shall be investigating that life outside school, of course. Indeed, we have already begun to do so. But if you know of any connections this girl may have had with either men or women, it is your duty to tell us about them. I need hardly remind you that this is not a routine death; we are directing a murder investigation."

"Yes. I'm aware of that, but I can tell you nothing that is helpful. I didn't teach the girl myself, though I did when she was lower down the school." She was tight-lipped now, suddenly careful. Then she smiled and said, "A Superintendent is rather a grand rank, isn't it? I thought you'd be desk-bound at CID headquarters, like a headmaster who is so busy administrating that he has no time to teach any more."

It was a blatant attempt to divert him from a particular line of questioning. He wondered for a moment if there was a little resentment of her own headmaster in the comparison. But she

29

was shrewd and correct: Lambert, in insisting on being out and about amid the suspects in any enquiry, was quite atypical of his rank. Commissioners and Chief Constables sometimes raised questions as well as eyebrows over it, but he survived because he got results. As long as he caught high-profile villains, he made other reputations as well as his own, and the hierarchy sanctioned his methods. He said gruffly, "I find I get the feel of a case better if I am in direct contact with those involved. Sometimes you read between the lines of what people say. Or hear between the words, I suppose I should say."

He looked a direct challenge at her, letting her know that the thought referred to her. But the moment when she had almost speculated about the dead girl's contacts was past. She said evenly, "I'll assemble a group of her close friends for you to talk to, but it will take a little time: they're all in different classes, you see. Could you see them at twelve o'clock? The sooner the better – this place will be rife with rumour once the kids pick up the fact that Alison was murdered."

"Indeed it will. We shall be as low-key as possible in our approach, but we shall also need to be as thorough as is necessary. We'll have to question anyone in the school who seems to have had a close connection with the dead girl. Male or female. Pupils or staff."

He hoped he might get a reaction to the last phrase, but Margaret Peplow looked thoughtfully at the rug between them on the polished floor. "Yes, I understand that. I'll try to get hold of anyone who might be helpful to you in the next couple of hours. But please remember that most of the people you will see are now well into their final year of A level studies, preparing for exams which will shape the rest of their lives. It is vital that that preparation is disrupted as little as possible."

"It will be, I can assure you. But the way to ensure that is for people to be as frank as possible from the start. Perhaps you would be good enough to convey that thought to the people you are going to get together for us."

She nodded, stood up as Hook shut his notebook, then realised she had anticipated the end of the interview. Her relief was transparent; Lambert studied it for a moment before he said,

"What do you know of the girl's relations with her parents, Mrs Peplow?"

She shrugged. "Mr Watts is a stepfather, I understand. I don't think we've ever seen him in the school. Mrs Watts came to some of the parent-teacher meetings. The last time I saw her was a couple of years ago. She's not particularly highly educated herself, but she seemed a caring mother, anxious to do the best possible things for her child. But you only see one dimension of parents, when you meet them to talk about their children's progress at school. It's a stress situation – on both sides sometimes, but in different ways." She smiled, happy to be on ground where she had the advantage of them.

"You say you never saw Mr Watts. Is that unusual?"

"No, not particularly. Lots of parents leave these meetings to one or the other: usually it's Mum who gets the short straw. In some cases, we don't see either of them for years. That's trouble, particularly with younger children: it usually gets through to the child that no one is particularly interested in his or her progress and behaviour."

"But Alison Watts was a good student?"

"Yes. Like almost everyone else, she had her distractions, over the years. But that's part of growing up. We teachers often assume that kids should perform at their optimum all the time, but it's part of human nature that they don't."

"But there was no dramatic falling away in the last few months?"

"No, I don't think so. We only have internal exams at the end of the first year sixth, but no one said they noticed anything dreadful. She wasn't brilliant, but she'd have made university all right, with a reasonable performance this year."

"And no traumas that you were aware of in her personal life?"

"No. We asked ourselves about that when she went missing, naturally, but we didn't turn up anything remarkable. Of course, young people of that age can be pretty clannish when it comes to concealing things. You may find them more forthcoming than they were to us, now that you're engaged upon a murder investigation."

31

Again it was a shrewd insight into their work. The worst crime of all carried with it a grisly glamour. People were fascinated by their involvement in an investigation, however peripheral. It made them more anxious to be helpful, to reveal as much as they could so as to retain their contact with the uneasy excitement of murder and violence. Lambert said, "We'll see the group you think were her particular friends together, initially. We'll give them the chance to speak to us individually afterwards, if they wish to. Did Alison have a steady boyfriend?"

"Yes. Jamie Allen. Nice lad." She looked for a moment as if she might comment on the relationship, then shut her lips firmly.

"We'll see him on his own, after the others, if you'd be good enough to arrange it. And the same with any individual members of staff who might have a particular insight into the girl's life."

"I doubt whether there are any of those." The denial came too quickly upon the question, as Lambert had felt it might. Then, as if she realised it and felt the need to extricate herself, Margaret Peplow said hastily, "I'll ask around, of course, but I doubt whether I'll come up with any member of staff for you."

It left Lambert more than ever convinced that there was such a person.

Men are forbidden visitors to hostels for battered wives. Understandably. Lambert took a female Detective Sergeant with him and let her do the talking.

DS Ruth David was an athletic, willowy thirty-year-old who looked as if she had never been hit in her life. That didn't endear her to the woman who opened the heavy Victorian wooden door six inches after inspecting their warrants at the eye-hole. "Mrs Watts ain't seein' no one," said this squat figure. "And we don't let men in here, anyway." She looked at Lambert as if she suspected him of fouling the doorstep.

"Nevertheless, we need to see her," said Ruth David calmly. "You can send her out here if you like, or we'll take her down to the station if we have to. But it would be better if we saw her inside your stronghold. I'm sure she'd feel safer there."

The door opened another inch, so that they got the full width of the guardian's scowl. "She ain't done nothing."

"We don't think she has, but we need her help."

"To put that bugger behind bars. That's what you need her help for."

"Perhaps. If he has damaged her, and she is prepared to bring charges, we may be able to do just that." Ruth David was well aware that it was usually the battered woman's reluctance to pursue matters through the courts that enabled the offender to escape justice.

Perhaps this sturdy sentry also knew about that. She opened the door another inch, then said with a nod at Lambert, "He can't come in 'ere. No way."

"I think he can. I understand your reservations, but on this occasion he must. Can you find us a room to talk? As near to the front door as you like, so long as it's private."

DS David accompanied the last sentence with her most confident smile, and the woman allowed them grudgingly to penetrate the outer recesses of her citadel. She led them into an office three yards from the thick front door and shut the door firmly upon them only when she saw Lambert safely seated, as though she was shutting in a dangerous dog. It was a room with a frayed Indian rug in the middle, a serviceable but ancient wooden desk, and three scratched filing cabinets which were obviously cast-offs from some more affluent office. Perhaps everything in this place was battered. Or perhaps, as seemed increasingly the case as the millennium approached, a necessary and worthy enterprise was starved of funds, was dependent on voluntary contributions for its upkeep and survival.

Katherine Mary Watts came into the room within a minute. Her hair was untidy, dropping in an unintended curtain over one side of her face until she tossed it aside. She had been crying, which is what they expected: it was little more than twelve hours since she had heard the news of her daughter's death from the WPC who had been dispatched hastily to the refuge when they heard of her presence there. Her eyes were puffed, her cheeks an unnatural, tear-washed red. But grief did not account for the ugly bruise and broken flesh on the side of her forehead, dangerously near her temple, nor the swollen, misshapen nose which she now dabbed with a fistful of tissues.

33

Lambert had risen when she entered, but he had more sense than to attempt any formal contact. He carefully avoided even moving forward to cut down the space between them. He sat down when the dead girl's mother sat. He could not but be aware of the contrast between this shabby, defeated figure and the cool and unforced beauty of Ruth David in her maroon top and slate-grey pleated skirt. Life rarely seemed fair in the manifestations it offered to him. He said formally, "You are Katherine Watts?"

"Yes. Kate. Everyone calls me Kate."

"Right. Kate it shall be."

She looked him in the face for the first time since she had come into the room, as if she took his friendliness as some kind of challenge. "I'm not going to bring a complaint against him, you know. He doesn't mean anything. Some of it's my fault, really."

Ruth David said quickly, "But it isn't, is it, Kate? People always say things like that to us. You should consider charging him, you know."

"No. He doesn't really mean anything. But when money's tight and the drink gets to him, he forgets himself. And I expect I nag him a bit. Some of it must be my fault."

"You don't really believe that, Kate, any more than I do. Did you hit *him*? Has *he* got a face knocked out of shape?"

It took another woman to be as impatient, as brutal about the results of violence, as this; Lambert would not have risked it, in this room where he felt like an interloper. Kate Watts's hand rose unthinkingly to the damage on her head as she shook it at her questioner, fingering the swelling near her temple, estimating the disfigurement with her fingers. Perhaps she had not dared to look in the mirror that day. She said wearily, "Just leave it, will you? We'll sort ourselves out. Robert's a good man, most of the time."

They had heard it too often for it to fill them with anything but despair. But there was nothing they could do to force the woman to face facts; far too often the Crown Prosecution Service spent days preparing an effective case in situations like this, only for it never to come to court when their chief witness withdrew at the eleventh hour. Sometimes, as it seemed to be in this case, it was through misguided loyalty, the mistaken belief in the hearts of many women that their patience and love could quell the violence in a man where others had failed. Sometimes it was merely fear that more and worse violence would result from any attempt to pursue things through the courts.

Lambert said quietly, "You need to consider what Detective Sergeant David is saying very carefully, Mrs Watts. But we are not here this morning to ask you for any statement about how you came to be in this place. We are here to talk to you about your daughter."

She looked at him again now, with wide, blue, tear-washed eyes. "Alison was murdered, wasn't she? I felt it from the start. I've become more certain with each week that's passed since she disappeared. She'd have been in touch otherwise. She wasn't the kind to go off without a word to her mother."

She seemed calm, even composed, despite her grief. They were going to be able to question her, when they had feared that she would be too distraught to make much sense. Lambert said, "I can understand that you feared she must be dead, when the weeks went past and you didn't hear from her. But why did you think she had been murdered, Kate?"

He had said it gently. But she looked for a moment like a cornered animal, as if she had been caught out in a mistake and now did not know where to turn. "I don't know why I said that. I – I suppose I just thought she might have been getting in with the wrong sort of people. Then, when she disappeared, and I had all those long hours during the nights to think about it, I suppose I feared the worst." She looked at him desperately, feeling incoherent, wondering whether her words made any kind of sense, wanting this man who listened so attentively to interrupt her, to say he understood, to smooth over her fears with consoling words. Since she had entered this hostel, everyone she had spoken to had been anxious only to reassure her, to convince her that the world was not as bad a place as it had appeared during the worst times outside.

Now she was facing the first male face she had seen for three days, lined and inquisitive, the grey eyes seeming to reach into her very soul. He did not speak, when she waited for him to do so, and she went on desperately, disjointedly, "Girls get secretive at Alison's age. She went out quite a lot – much more than she used to. And I didn't always know where she was, especially at the weekends. I suppose it made me imagine all kinds of things were going on. But probably they weren't. But Alison was almost a young woman, you know. And educated. Quite leaving her old mum behind."

She gave them an involuntary, unexpected smile on that thought. Then tears sprang searingly to her eyes and she dabbed again with her tissues at the red, sore cheeks beneath them. Lambert had the ruthlessness of the long-term CID man. Distress made a woman vulnerable: she might reveal things in her anguish that she would hide when she was in control of herself. He said calmly, "Who do you think might have killed Alison, Mrs Watts?"

"No one. I shouldn't have said that. I don't know why I did."

"Because someone did. You were the one who was right in your fears when she was missing, you see. Someone had killed her. And I'm sure you are more anxious than anyone that we should bring the person who killed your daughter to justice."

"Yes. Yes I am. Yes, of course."

In her distraction, she spoke like one anxious to convince herself. She stared down at her shoes. They saw that her hair, which must once have been bright red, even carroty, was grey over an inch up from its roots. She must have been pretty once, in a round-faced, snub-nosed way. Carefree as a doll, thought Lambert. Now that nose was distorted and swollen, and he had been glad when she gave that fleeting smile to see that she had a full set of undamaged teeth. He said inexorably, "Then you must tell us about anyone who you think might have done harm to your daughter, Kate. He might not have meant to kill her: something might have gone wrong. Or he might have panicked and done more harm than he intended to her. Lots of murders come when people panic."

He had deliberately let the killer be a male. It seemed an appropriate presumption, in this of all places, and the victim's mother made no attempt to question it. "Yes. Yes, I suppose so. But I can't help you. Perhaps if you talk to her friends, they'll be able to tell you more about the people she went about with."

"We've already arranged to see the people who were closest to her at school." He looked at his watch. "That will be in about an hour. Is there anyone else you think we should see? Think carefully, please."

She hadn't mentioned her husband since their opening exchanges, and he was interested to see that she didn't consider him now. "No. No, I can't think of anyone. She had a boy friend at the school. But Jamie wouldn't hurt anyone. He was as upset as we were when she went missing."

"We shall be seeing him, though. Just in case he can suggest any line of enquiry to us. Like you."

She nodded, but made no further comment on the boy friend. Lambert said, "I think you told us earlier that she was going out a lot more than she used to. Perhaps because she felt herself almost a woman, as you say. Have you any idea where she went on these occasions?"

"No."

"Or whom she met?"

"No . . . She was a bit secretive about it, if you must know."

"I'm afraid we must, Kate, now that this is a murder enquiry. And I have to ask you the next question, too. Had your daughter ever had any involvement that you are aware of with illegal drugs?"

"No. Well, she said a year or two ago that cannabis should be made legal, and we had a bit of an up-and-downer about it. But that's normal for young people, isn't it? I'm sure she never took anything. We'd have known about it if she had, I'm sure."

The two CID officers had heard such sentiments too often to set much store by them. Probably they meant no more than that the girl had not brought drugs into her home. But no doubt they would be clearer when they had spoken with her contemporaries. Ruth David said softly, "Do you have an up-to-date photograph of your daughter, Kate?"

She nodded, then rummaged swiftly through her possessions in the shopping bag at her feet. The print was a seven inch by five inch enlargement of a snap. It was still in its frame, but the

37

glass was cracked, making them wonder if it had been damaged in the clash between husband and wife that had sent Katherine Watts here. DS David, anxious to keep the level of emotion at a minimum, put it away with scarcely a glance. "Thank you. We'll let you have it back in due course."

"It's the last one," the mother said. "Robert took it in the back garden. It must have been about a month before – before she went."

Lambert could see the woman getting exhausted before his eyes. They could not press her much further. But there was one area they must explore, however briefly. He said, "What sort of relationship did Alison have with her stepfather, Kate?"

She glanced up at him sharply, then knuckled her hands fiercely together over the tissues in her lap. "They loved each other, didn't they? Don't let anyone tell you any different from that." She paused for his challenge, but he said nothing, and after a moment she floundered on, repeating herself, becoming ever less coherent. "He adopted her properly, you know, when we got married eight years ago. They loved each other: 'course, they had their rows with each other, but what teenage girl doesn't fight with her dad? She used to come in late sometimes, and my Robert got upset with her, but that's only what you'd have to expect. She gave us things to put up with, and no mistake, at times, did Ally. But nothing you wouldn't expect, I suppose."

Ruth David looked at Lambert, received the tiniest of nods, and turned to look Kate Watts in the face from no more than four feet. "You're in here because Robert knocked you about, aren't you, Kate? We're all agreed on that. We're not here to follow that up, as Superintendent Lambert has told you, but I have to ask you this: did your husband ever strike Alison?"

"No!" It was almost a shout, lifting her off the old Windsor chair on which she had perched throughout. "No, you mustn't think that. Well, he may have given her the odd slap on the leg years ago, when she was about eleven or twelve, but nothing more than that. You mustn't think that Robert ever ill-treated my girl, you mustn't. I told you, they loved each other!"

In these days when the police unearthed more and more sexual abuse, it wasn't the wisest phrase to keep repeating about a girl and her stepfather. But clearly Kate Watts thought that whatever her husband had done to her, he had had a normal relationship with her dead daughter.

They left her then. She went with them to the door and took the arm of the younger woman as they turned to leave. she said, "Get them for me, won't you? Whoever did this dreadful thing to Alison. Make sure you get them for me."

As they got into the car, they saw her strained, tear-stained face with its livid bruise staring down at them from an upper window, a reminder to them in the days to come of a mother's cry for justice.

Chapter Six

LAMBERT dropped off at home for coffee, leaving Ruth David to go back to the station and feed their findings from the refuge into Rushton's computer. Coffee at home was an indulgence only possible because his wife now worked part instead of full time at the primary school where she had taught for the last ten years.

Christine knew that he had a murdered girl to investigate, a corpse too old to offer many forensic clues, a murder hunt that was severely handicapped from the outset by beginning twelve weeks after the event. At one time she would have known none of these things. John Lambert would have hugged these facts like the rest of the job close against him, excluding her from the horrors as well as the rewards of his work. Those days when they had almost split up seemed now to belong to another world.

"How was it?" she said as she set the steaming aromatic coffee in front of him. For she knew also that he had been to see the mother of the dead girl; knew how she herself would feel if one of her daughters had been killed at eighteen by person or persons unknown.

He shrugged. "We got as far as we'd any right to expect, at this stage. Perhaps further," he said. "I still haven't got a very clear picture of the dead girl, but I'm seeing some of her school friends in half an hour. That should help."

"I think I taught Alison Watts when she was nine years old," said Christine Lambert quietly.

She had found a class photograph from the primary school, with a group of smiling children and a teacher standing at each end of the rows. Lambert saw his own wife ten years ago, still a bright, energetic woman with an alert, humorous smile and glossy hair. Now, nine short years later, she had lost a breast to a

40

mastectomy and was beginning HRT to counteract the brittleness of ageing bones. Age crept up on you, overtook you whilst you were busy elsewhere. Before he knew it, he would be retired and tending the traditional policeman's roses. He had better get Bert Hook to swallow the golfing bug quickly; but that might be a greater challenge even than solving this murder.

Christine's neat, clear-varnished nail ran along the row of young faces and stopped at one in the middle. "That's her," she said.

He saw a slightly bewildered, pig-tailed girl with a brace on her teeth and her arms not quite folded in time for the camera, which had clearly caught her by surprise. There was nothing to distinguish her from the other children in the picture, unless you looked with a parent's biased eye. He pulled out the photograph that Kate Watts had given them, with its cheap frame and curiously pathetic cracked glass. The girl there was carefully made up, with fine brown hair which fell in shining natural waves over her temples. She wore a bright green silk blouse and was pretty, strikingly so, even with the end of a line of washing in the adjoining garden edging into the picture. There seemed no connection with the gauche little girl in the primary school group; this was a woman, conscious of the effect of her composed smile and her laughing, teasing eyes.

Christine Lambert looked at the photograph for a moment without speaking. It was difficult to comprehend that this creature, so full of life, so fully into living, was now no more than the lump of rotting flesh which had been retrieved from the Wye. She had been wrong to think she understood how the mother felt: you couldn't know what it was like to lose a child like that, she decided, unless it actually happened to you, however much you wanted to be sympathetic. It was one of those things so awful that even the most vivid imagination came nowhere near to experience.

She said only, "You'd have been better off if she'd been ugly, John. A girl like that is going to have excited lots of men."

Lambert took Hook with him to see the friends of Alison Watts. In his pre-CID days, Bert had gone into schools a lot, instructing young children in bicycle safety and older ones about the dangers of the developing drug culture. Older children still remembered him unexpectedly, sometimes at awkward times.

The two large men were followed by whisperings and curious looks as they went through the school playground and entered the sixth form complex. It had not taken long for news of the investigation to fly round the school community. Margaret Peplow met them as they stepped through the double glass doors. "I've put the girls in my office," she said. "It will be a bit of a squash in there, but you'll have complete privacy."

Lambert had expected a mixed group, but apparently the group closest to the dead girl had all been girls. And it was a bit of a squash, as they had been warned. The room had been set up with seats for the two policemen behind the desk; a group of six stand chairs had been brought in and arranged in a tight semi-circle in the rest of the room. A hush fell as sharply as a guillotine upon the high-pitched exchanges as the two men were ushered into the room. Six pairs of eyes turned expectantly to meet them. There was a strong smell of cheap perfume as they picked their way to the chairs behind the desk. There was also an excitement in the crowded room that they could almost feel. A sense of importance, of being involved in a great local event. And a touch of apprehension, even outright fear of what was to come.

"Most of you have probably already talked to a police officer when Alison Watts disappeared," said Lambert when he had introduced himself and Hook to the girls. "But this is altogether more serious. As I am sure Mrs Peplow has told you, we are now engaged upon a murder investigation. What we have to do is to build up a picture of a dead girl whom none of my team yet knows, but whom you all knew very well. We need your help. We need to know the kind of girl Alison Watts was, both in school and out of it. We need to know what her likes and dislikes were, how she behaved, how she thought, the people she knew. Even the people she didn't know or hardly knew, if they had any sort of interest in her. I need hardly say that you mustn't hold anything back, however trivial it may seem, however embarrassing it might appear for someone. No one who isn't guilty of a crime is going to suffer from anything you tell us, and whatever you say now will be treated in confidence. I should like you also to maintain discretion about anything which passes between us, in here or elsewhere."

42

He had their attention. The room was so quiet that it was almost oppressive. He said, "We can start with some easy facts. Will someone tell me what subjects Alison was studying for her A levels?"

The tension slackened. The girl nearest to him, tall and thin, with the horn-rimmed glasses which were now fashionable among the young, said, "That's easy, at any rate. Alison was doing English, History and Sociology."

The girl next to her, anxious to get in now, said, "She started off last year doing English, History and French, but she dropped French after a few weeks because she found it hard going. She switched to Sociology because we all think it's a bit of an easy option, you see!"

There was a collective nervous giggle at this daring public voicing of a view they had agreed upon among themselves. Lambert smiled. "One of my own daughters decided that, in this very school. About eight years ago, now. It worked out all right for her."

The girl, thus emboldened, went on, "Ally wanted to read English at university. Or perhaps English and Drama, if she could get in at Bristol."

Hook wrote down the names of the teachers who were mainly responsible for teaching Alison in these subjects. It was all routine, factual stuff. It meant work, of course: a member of the CID team would have to see all of these people individually in due course, searching for the one suggestive fact that might provide a clue to the mystery of this intelligent girl's death. But it was necessary information, and it got the girls talking, even anxious to contribute something which might draw them into the grisly glamour of a murder investigation. They wrote down other names: pupils who had had some sort of close connection but were not in this room. A girl with whom Alison had been on a brief holiday, two years earlier. A boy with a motorbike, who had taken Alison for spins out into the Cotswolds; he had left the school a year ago after his GCSEs but still kept in touch with her.

They even managed a few collective giggles about life in the school, a few bold phrases about the deficiencies of the people who taught them. Then Lambert said, "Everyone has a life outside this place as well. Particularly you sixth formers. It's right and proper that you should. We know that, and we want to know – need to know – everything about the life that Alison Watts had outside Oldford Comprehensive."

A sudden collective silence, such as there had been when they first came into the room. That was not a bad sign; it probably meant that there were useful things someone here could tell them.

The girls shifted uneasily, wanting to look at each other, conscious that in this crowded, claustrophobic room they could not do so without giving things away. A girl at the end of the little half-circle of chairs, who had been happy to talk about Alison's progress in her studies, looked quickly at her neighbour, a pretty dark-haired girl who had so far said less than anyone. It was enough to make Lambert chance his arm. He spoke directly to the dark-haired girl. "Ally went about with you quite a bit when you were away from the school, didn't she? What kind of things did you do in your leisure time?"

"Not a lot, in the last few months before she disappeared. We went to the discos in Oldford on Saturday nights sometimes, but other girls here went to those as well."

A girl at the other end of the line of chairs said, "Ally seemed to have given up going, though. She hadn't been for over a year, I think." She looked along the line to the girl Lambert had first singled out. "You knew her best, Judith. Didn't you go into Gloucester and Cheltenham with her sometimes?"

"Not in the last few months I didn't." It was a hasty denial. She looked back at Lambert and at Hook with his notebook and his busy ballpen. "Ally did go into Cheltenham and Gloucester, but not with me. Not in the months before she died." She was very insistent, seemed almost relieved to see Hook recording her statement.

Lambert looked along the line of girls. "Does anyone know where she went to on these occasions?"

There was a collective shaking of heads. A girl in the centre said, "We didn't see as much of her in the summer term as we used to, I think." She looked round and the heads which had just shaken now nodded in unison. She hesitated, then said, "Allie was a bit older than most of us. A bit more sophisticated than me, certainly, if I'm honest. And she had more money than most of us."

The girls looked at the floor, but no one contradicted her. This was something none of the CID team had heard about the girl, so far, and it interested Hook in particular. The house in which he had talked to the girl's stepfather had not seemed a rich one. And Bert would have bet the boots he no longer wore that Robert Watts did not earn a lot, and that most of what he had to spare passed across the counter of a bar or a betting shop. He said quietly, "And where did this money come from? Does anybody know?"

They looked at each other again, each one seeming reluctant to speak. Eventually the girl who had voiced the thought said, "None of us knew that. We speculated about it a bit, among ourselves, when she appeared in clothes we'd have killed for, but she never gave us any hints."

There was a subdued, collective giggle; there was no humour in it, merely an involuntary nervous release. What had been no more than routine gossip in a tight community had acquired an extra significance with the death of the subject. Hook said, "Did Alison have a weekend job?"

They looked again at the pretty, dark-haired girl, who blushed as she said, "No. We used to work together in the Budgens supermarket on Saturday mornings until about a year ago. I still do, but Ally gave up about the time when we went into the sixth form."

"Yet you all think she had money from somewhere. You must have some idea where it came from."

There were muttered denials amidst a sporadic shaking of heads. An uneasiness hung now in the room, but no one was willing to voice a thought about the source of the girl's affluence. Hook eventually said, "Well, it's something we shall need to find out about. If any one of you has a thought about it, please contact us immediately. We'll give you a number when we leave here."

Lambert said, "You've had contacts with the drug culture, of course. All young people have. We're not here today to talk about drugs, except as they may affect a murder investigation. What can you tell me about Alison Watts's connections with drugs?"

There was a long, uneasy silence. "Don't trust the pigs" was the watchword they had been given in the discos and pubs, and

45

it was a slogan which sprang easily enough to their naive young lips. But these two earnest policemen were the reality, individuals rather than the collective filth their contemporaries went on about so glibly. And they were investigating the death of a girl who had sat with them for years as they moved up the classrooms of the school, who had laughed with them, schemed with them, shared their secrets. The girl with the horn-rimmed glasses took a deep breath and said, "Most of us have tried cannabis at one time or another. It was offered fairly openly around the school, about two years ago."

The girl next to her said hastily, "But it isn't now. And most of us only tried pot once, or perhaps twice." Plainly she feared that this collective confession might be relayed to someone in authority, probably a parent.

Lambert smiled; a grim, knowing smile. "Did Alison ever take anything stronger? Ecstasy, for instance?"

If she had possessed drugs, she might have dealt in them, made her money from dealing. It would be her likeliest contact with the violence that always lurked around serious criminal money. But the dark-haired girl who seemed to have been closest to their murder victim said, "We never saw her with anything, did we, girls?" and looked round to receive their nods of confirmation.

Lambert said drily, "But by your own accounts, you didn't see her much at weekends in the last year or so before she died. The period which most interests us. Now, bear with me just a little longer, because we're coming to the end. We know Alison was murdered. We don't know as yet whether there was any sexual aspect to her killing, but you're not stupid, any of you. You know as well as I do that the overwhelming majority of killings of young women in circumstances like this are committed by men: probably more than ninety-five per cent. So I must ask you to treat this last question very seriously. We know about Jamie Allen: we shall be seeing him soon. There is no suggestion that Jamie had any personal connection with this death, but we hope that like you he may be able to suggest some avenues of enquiry to us. What I am asking you is whether you know of any other men who had a connection with Alison. You've already told us about the lad with the motor-bike, for instance. Are there any others?"

46

The girls looked collectively at the rug, as if its design was suddenly of overriding interest. Lambert said, as determinedly low-key as he could keep it, "Were there any older men with whom Alison had any kind of connection? Not necessarily a lasting relationship – some much looser connection may still turn out to be significant."

Another long, agonising silence. Then the dark girl said in a clear, small voice, "No. Nothing serious. We all had schoolgirl crushes, when we were younger. They don't count. I'm sure Ally didn't have any affairs with older men in the months before she died. Nothing we know about, anyway."

There was a low murmur of approval after her last phrase, which took the responsibility of knowledge away from them. There was something here, Lambert was sure. But he felt a collective closing of the ranks. If they were to tease out any more information, it would need to be with individuals, not in the atmosphere of febrile excitement and group loyalty which now prevailed in this room.

He sent the girls on their way, then sat for a few minutes with Hook. "Schoolgirl crushes," he quoted thoughtfully. "They're usually harmless: I remember my own daughters going through the phase ten years and more ago. But they can become something more serious, sometimes, if the teacher allows himself or herself to get involved." He looked at the list of subjects that Alison Watts had been studying, and their teachers. "I wonder if metaphysical poetry is on the English syllabus this year," he mused.

Hook felt a quotation hanging over him, but his Open University arts courses hadn't included the metaphysical poets. He looked appropriately puzzled: Superintendents had to be indulged. Lambert said:

" 'Had we but world enough and time,
This coyness, lady, were no crime . . .
But at my back I always hear
Time's wingèd chariot hurrying near . . .
Now therefore, while the youthful hue
Sits on thy skin like morning dew,
And while thy willing soul transpires

47

At every pore with instant fires,
Now let us sport us while we may . . .' "

"It's a good chat-up line," conceded Hook reluctantly.

"Andrew Marvell," said Lambert dreamily. "He knew a thing or two, the old boy. Used to use that poem myself as a seduction technique, in the old days."

"Worked for you, did it? Left with their drawers in their handbags, did they?"

"Don't be coarse, Bert. It's all a long time ago. What I'm saying is that the English master has the glories of literature at his disposal to persuade a girl into bed. Or for the girl to persuade herself."

Hook said dubiously, "It's worth a try, I suppose. Ingenious, anyway."

"Thank you, Sergeant. Not as ingenious as you think, though; there are other indications. I've looked at the staff lists. The lady who teaches history is a Miss Haylett. She taught my own daughters years ago; she's sixty-two and an archetypal spinster. The sociology is shared by two married women who job-share."

The light dawned on Bert. "And the English teacher?"

"Jason Bullimore. Twenty-nine. Single. Has a first in English Literature. Therefore probably randy." Lambert paraded his prejudice with an unashamed flourish.

Chapter Seven

THE large board near the gates carried the name of the school and beneath it in letters almost as large, the legend 'Headmaster, Mr T H Murray, MA, FRSA'. They were admiring the gold lettering on the dark green background when a voice hailed them from behind. It was the head himself, rather breathless after chasing them across the playground of his school. "Hope you got the cooperation you wanted," he said.

Lambert smiled, "Yes, sir. Both Mrs Peplow and your sixth formers have been most helpful. It's early days yet, of course, but one or two lines of enquiry have already suggested themselves." Keep the buggers guessing was always a sound principle, even when they were anxious headmasters. Especially then, he decided.

Murray looked dismayed for a moment. Then he said, with a brightness donned as obviously as a hat, "I'm glad to hear that. The sooner this matter is cleared up the better, for all concerned. I understand why you have to begin your work here with Alison's friends, but I'm sure in my own mind that you'll find the murderer has nothing to do with my school."

"Really, sir. Have you any reason for saying that?"

"Oh, no! No, not at all. It's just – just what I suppose you'd call a gut feeling. I suppose when you've laboured for years to build something up and you're proud of it, you don't believe that anything as awful as this could have any connection with it."

"Yes, sir, we understand that. 'Murder should take place on the sidewalk,' someone once said. An American fiction-writer, I believe. Meaning it should confine itself to squalid city pavements, I suppose. We find increasingly that it doesn't. Poor Alison found that out."

"Yes." It was bewildering to have policemen quoting Raymond

Chandler at him: somehow he hadn't expected such men to be literate. "Well, I have to respect your experience, of course. But Alison was an attractive girl. And – well, lively."

"Lively, sir?" Lambert found he was quite enjoying himself. The headmaster was not used to having his words weighed so carefully by others. He was beginning to wish he had left well alone instead of trying to find out how things were going. "Yes. If that's the right word. She was an outgoing girl, Alison, as well as attractive. And she liked men." He blurted out the last phrase, abandoning his diversions, wishing fervently now that he had never embarked on this.

Lambert swung round to face him directly; the movement seemed to threaten that he might after all not leave the school premises. "Liked men more than most girls, did she, Mr Murray? Are you suggesting she was something of a nyphomaniac?"

"Oh, no, nothing like that! Certainly not!" Lurid headlines ran before the head's wide, panic-filled eyes. "It's just that she was an attractive girl, and conscious of it. She seemed to like men, and to be aware of her charms. Perhaps she didn't always repel their advances, when she might have been better to do so." A prick-teaser, he wanted to say, but you couldn't use a phrase like that. Not here. He waited for a reaction; the two large men merely looked at him steadily. He added hastily, "Of course, that's just an impression I had. I may be quite wrong, But I thought you should know, that's all. I'm sure there were men in her life whom none of us know about."

"That's really most illuminating, sir. Thank you for being so frank. Though it doesn't make our job any easier if you're right, of course. The wider the circle of her acquaintances, the wider the net we shall have to cast."

Suddenly, Tom Murray felt that he did not want the net to be cast too widely. "Yes. Well, I just thought it possible that she had been killed by some man after a random meeting or a first date. Someone she hardly knew, who thought he could go as far as he wanted, and didn't like it when she tried to stop him."

"That's always possible, of course, sir. Though killings by an assailant totally unknown to the victim are a tiny minority of the total."

"Really? Yes, I suppose that would be so. Well, I thought it would be worth airing the thought, in case you hadn't picked it up from anyone else." Having rushed to catch the CID men, Murray was now wondering desperately how he could end an exchange he wished he had never begun.

"It's most useful to have your thoughts, sir. And may I compliment you on your knowledge of your pupils. It can't be easy to have observed one girl so closely, when you have nine hundred pupils in the school to worry about."

That thought visibly discomforted Thomas Murray, MA, FRSA. They revolved it in their minds as they walked slowly to the car.

Superintendent and sergeant drove in silence for two miles. The road ran away past the school playing fields, with their hockey and rugby posts and shrill-voiced, bright-shirted children in pursuit of a soccer ball, on into the Gloucestershire countryside, which was still a luxuriant green despite the tints of orange and yellow on the leaf-laden trees. Like many CID men, they did not need small talk, and they had worked together now for far too long to feel that silences needed to be broken. Each was busy with his own thoughts, each digesting the teeming evidence of the day so far.

Eventually, as they crested a hill and ran towards a long white building in the valley below, Lambert said, "A basket of balls!"

"Oh, I don't think it's as bad as that," said Hook evenly. "We're beginning to make progress. If we—"

"Not the case, Bert. As you well know. We need to hit some golf balls. A basket of fifty each, at the range. Well worth a few quid, for the sheer release it gives. Clear the mind, it will. Blow away the cobwebs!" He turned his old Vauxhall Senator between the high gateposts and drove over the gravel to park behind the pro's shop.

"Not golf, John. Anything but that!" Hook buried his face in his hands in mock horror. "We haven't time. This is our first full day on a murder enquiry."

"And we shall be at it until ten o'clock tonight, if I'm any judge," said Lambert firmly. "Twenty minutes with a 7-iron is just what you need. And I just happen to have that very club from

51

your set in my boot. You left it beside the eighteenth green at the golf club when we finished your last learning experience."

Bert slumped dismally in his seat. "It's a conspiracy," he said glumly.

In two minutes, they were hitting golf balls from adjoining booths on the range. Lambert produced several satisfactory shots, as he often seemed to do when there was no audience to applaud his efforts. He listened with a widening smile to the rising tide of language from the normally placid Hook on the other side of the five foot high partition.

Bert was concentrating with increasing fury on the elusive golf balls around his feet. A 7-iron should be an easy club to use. The fact that Lambert had told him that added to his problems and his rage. He topped three at empts in succession, then was aghast to hear himself as he sent his next lurching contact away with the deperate injunction to "Get down there, you blasted, bloody, bleeding thing!"

Lambert put his elbows on top of the division between them, the better to study his sergeant's swing. "Rhythm's the thing, Bert. As in many other pleasurable things," he said quietly. He didn't mind interrupting his practice to give the benefit of his long experience to a beginner, he decided.

Bert Hook, who had not realised that his efforts were being observed, started violently. He gave the super a withering look, then turned back to the mat and the cluster of grey-white balls with what dignity he could muster. "Building up the tension, this is, not getting rid of it," he grumbled darkly. He swung desperately at a ball, only half-topped it, achieved his best contact yet, watched it slice away to the right, and was appalled to hear his old friend tut-tutting behind him.

"Slicing still, I see. And bending your left arm. And swaying. And letting your head move," said Lambert magisterially. It was really quite consoling to see such elementary mistakes. It made you realise how far you had progressed from your tentative early steps in the game. Sometimes you thought you had learned nothing, but when you saw a real beginner like Bert struggling to hit the ball, you had to accept that you had acquired a fair degree of proficiency over the years. And Bert was no stooge at sport: he had been an excellent cricketer, up to minor counties standard; had opened the bowling for Herefordshire in his palmy days, and taken many good wickets. Yet here he was struggling, even losing his rag with the game; it really was quite consoling.

"You're snatching from the top again," Lambert said helpfully, "and looping your swing so that you come across the ball. Adjust your stance a little and try to come at it from the inside."

Bert said something which was fortunately indistinguishable. He shut his eyes as he tried to knock Lambert's succession of comments into his raging brain. When he opened his eyes, the ball was still there, midway between his feet staring insolently up at him, defying him to direct the blow which would kill it at the back of its neck. He adjusted his stance a little, straightened his left arm rigidly towards the ball, dropped his head to look at the back of it like an inquisitive bird.

"That's better!" said Lambert approvingly from behind him. "Now, remember to swing the clubhead back slowly, and we're in business. In your own time, then!" he said with breezy cheerfulness. It was important to be not just well-informed but encouraging when you gave instruction: his wife had told him that.

Hook felt like Quasimodo on a bad day. For a moment, he thought he could not move the club at all from this awful, contrived position. Then he turned his wide shoulders with a huge effort, twisting his body like an arthritic crab. At the top of his swing, he fixed the ball with a wide, malevolent left eye, feeling again like the legendary Charles Laughton; for an awful moment, the impulse to launch his downswing by shouting "The bells!" hammered through his head. Instead, he threw himself at the ball with a huge grunt and a desperate unwinding of his tortured arms.

He hit the mat two inches behind the ball, with an impact that shuddered his own booth and the two on either side of it. The head of his 7-iron bounced upwards, brushing the very top of the ball. It trickled forward some two feet, seemingly in deference to the immense effort Hook had applied rather than from any definite contact. The unseen presence behind him tut-tutted again. "You need to relax to hit the ball properly," said Lambert helpfully.

Hook hated him with the unswerving, undiluted hate a child in darkness has for a witch. This man had taken advantage of his rank to bring him here against his will and torture him. "Blast the bastard, fucking thing!" he said. "And you too! Blast and damn the whole fucking issue." He concentrated all of his fury on the ball which had so mocked him, imprinting Lambert's features on the curved surface which faced him. Then he moved forward swiftly, as if he hoped to catch it by surprise, and launched himself at it with every ounce of his remaining energy.

He should have missed it altogether, allowing Lambert to counsel again the virtues of control and the steady head. Perhaps some merciful providence intervened to avoid needless bloodshed on this balmy autumn afternoon. For the face of the 7-iron contacted the ball at the bottom of its mighty swing and the ball flew away in a massive, impossible parabola, pitching near and running past the 150-yard marker post on the ball-littered grass before them. "Take that!" yelled Hook. "Take that, you rotten bastard!" He was not sure whether he was shouting at the distant ball or at his mentor. He found that the blood was pounding in his head and he was breathing very hard. There was the odd spot dancing before his vision and he needed to stand with feet well apart to recover himself, mentally and physically. He did not dare to turn round.

Lambert felt he should offer some sort of congratulation on this fortunate blow of his sergeant's. But something warned him to be cautious. In ten years of working with Hook in a service noted for the vigour of its language, he had never heard him use the f-word before. Bert was a man almost unique in his placidity. Yet now, in a place of relaxation, with a tutor who could scarcely be more patient or understanding, he had completely lost control of himself. John Lambert shook his head sadly. Some instinct of self-preservation made him say nothing and resume the hitting of his own remaining golf balls.

Neither of them looked at the other until both the baskets of balls were exhausted. Bert was breathing hard, but neither success nor failure brought any further verbal reaction from him. Lambert hit one or two excellent shots, but found it difficult to concentrate. They dropped the empty wire baskets back by the ball-dispensing machine and strode silently back to the car. Then the old Vauxhall made its stately way back over four miles of winding roads to the murder room which had been set up at Oldford CID. Not a word was exchanged in the fourteen minutes of the journey.

Golf, they say, is a wonderful game for cementing friendships.

Jamie Allen had seen the two men come into the school, had seen them enter the head's room immediately after assembly. He had been the only person in the sixth form common room, hunched with a book in the corner, unnoticed by Mrs Peplow as she had led the two tall men through it and into her office. He had listened in trepidation to the low murmur of conversation in the long minutes which followed, unable to distinguish a single word. He had heard the excited talk at morning break; watched the girls assembled for the meeting with the CID men at midday – at 'high noon', as one of them had nervously called it. Munching his lunch-time sandwiches alone, he had watched from the library window as Mr Murray, the head teacher of the school, had run after the men to engage them in conversation at the school gates.

Being still seventeen, he had speculated about what all these people had said to the detectives about him, and about his relationship with Alison Watts. And all day he had waited for them to come for him, to take him away, to question him in the high-walled interview room at the station which he had seen in so many television police dramas. Yet all day no one had come to him, no message had arrived that he was to be questioned by those ominous, dark-suited men.

When four o'clock came, he found that he did not wish to leave the school. It was an anti-climax, this. He hung about the sixth form complex, unable to believe that even now someone would not tell him that he was urgently required. When she had first gone missing all those weeks ago, he had been the first person the police had spoken to about Alison. Yet today all these other people had been seen, had been asked about Alison, and he, who knew her best of all, had been ignored. At the beginning of the day he had felt apprehensive; now he felt both exhausted with the waiting and insulted that he should be given such low priority.

Jamie lived only threequarters of a mile from the school, on the same side of the market town. He had no bus to catch, like those who came from further afield in the school's wide rural catchment area. Without any deadline of this kind, he felt curiously listless and deflated. He had expected the police to provide the programme for his day, and they had let him down. For the first time, his active imagination began to toy with the idea that they had left him alone deliberately, left him to stew in his own juice, as his father put it when he became impatient with him, so that he might be more receptive to their methods, whatever they might be. It was not a pleasant idea.

Apart from the people who stayed on after school for the various clubs, most people had left the premises by the time he wandered across the concrete acreage of the playground, swinging his heavy briefcase gently, and moved with his gangling walk through the gates and away from the school. Most pupils, that is; from an oblique angle beside the window of the staffroom, Jamie's English teacher, Jason Bullimore, watched the tardy departure of his brightest pupil and speculated on what the lad was going through. As far as he knew, the police hadn't questioned Jamie yet. He wondered exactly what he would tell them, when they did.

She was trouble, that Alison Watts. Jail bait, for a man on the threshold of a fine career. He should have known it from the start, with his experience. For the hundredth time in the last few months, Jason Bullimore wished that he had never set eyes on the girl.

Chapter Eight

SCENE of Crime team, they called it. That was a misnomer, really: they were searching the dead girl's room, and in all probability that was not the scene of the crime. In all probability; that was all they could say at this stage. Keep an open mind, Lambert had warned them at the meeting, and Bert Hook had added that the girl's father seemed a dodgy character, who would stand watching.

So Sergeant Johnson and his team searched diligently at Number One, The Lawns. Murder investigations are infrequent in a provincial force, even in today's violent times. They carry an extra excitement, even for grizzled professionals like Jack Johnson, and most of his team were still junior enough to dream of making a reputation through the discovery of some significant item in the house that others had overlooked. Not even the laziest policeman was likely to treat a house search in a murder enquiry lightly, with the grisly example of Fred West in nearby Gloucester now built into every training scheme.

Experience told Johnson one thing at a glance. The girl's room was too tidy for them to expect much from it. It might be what you would expect with a girl gone missing eleven weeks ago, but it wasn't helpful. The carpet had been thoroughly vacuumed; nevertheless, he set two of his team to work on hands and knees, working methodically over every square foot in search of hairs, fibres, any small, overlooked, and just possibly significant items of detritus from the people who had been in this room. There was always the possibility that they would find something beneath the bed or around the feet of the wardrobe, areas which notoriously escaped the attentions of the upright vacuum.

A moment's careful inspection of the bed linen showed that it had been thoroughly laundered in the weeks since the girl's

57

departure. No chance of semen traces, no prospect of sweat or hair dropped in the extremes of passion. But they parcelled the blankets and sheets up for the forensic boys to inspect. With the advent of DNA testing, science could work new wonders. And it was a fair bet that the blankets at least had not been washed.

Robert Watts stood in the doorway of the bedroom, watching their actions with a grim smile which developed into a sneer as they proceeded. Many officers would have asked him to withdraw. The experienced Johnson was happy to see him there. Whilst apparently ignoring him, he watched for any reaction which might reveal more than the man realised. Watts might be just anti-police, as he had seemed from the moment when they had come into the square, cheerless house. But he might be a man with things to hide, a man who knew more about the disappearance of his stepdaughter than he had chosen to reveal. It was a bonus to have him under observation as they inspected the place where the girl had spent most of her hours in this house.

"You'll find nothing here," he said truculently, as the two young constables got up from their floor search with nothing but a paper clip and two tiny pieces of gravel in their small trays.

"Maybe not," said Johnson equably. "But you wouldn't forgive us, Mr Watts, if we weren't properly thorough, would you? Not when we're looking for something which might lead us to Alison's murderer."

Watts stared at him suspiciously. It seemed to dawn on him that a different, more helpful attitude would be appropriate in these circumstances, but he had little idea of how to present it. "You won't find anything that helps you here," he said. "You want to look in other places than here, instead of wasting all this time."

"Like where, Mr Watts? We're open to suggestions."

"Well, like around the town. Start with the people who taught her. And have a go at that tosspot of a boyfriend of hers, I should think. But you're the ones who're supposed to know. You're the clever buggers who're supposed to have a routine for these things."

"Yes, we are. And yes, we have. And the routine begins here, Mr Watts. With you, if you like. Have you any reason to suspect that the people you've just mentioned were involved in Alison's death?"

Apprehension flashed for a moment across his face before it turned surly. "Your job, that is, not mine. All I said is you should be getting on with it."

"And someone is, Mr Watts. Be assured of that. Just the same as someone saw your wife this morning. The routine you mentioned is in operation."

He had started at the mention of his wife. He did not ask where she was, though. He must have known that she was at the refuge all along, though he had denied that knowledge to Bert Hook when he had come to this house to tell him that Alison had been murdered. Now he was merely surprised that they had got to her so quickly.

Johnson looked round the small, rectangular room where Alison Watts had slept. "Very bare, for the room of a teenage girl, this is," he said. It wasn't clear whether he was addressing his staff in the room or Watts in the doorway. "Usually the walls are covered with posters. Pop stars for girls, footballers for boys."

"Took 'em down, didn't we?" said Watts. He was chewing now. Johnson was sure he hadn't unwrapped any gum. He must have had the stuff in his mouth all the time, but only renewed his chewing when he began to feel confident. Or wanted to look confident. Johnson nodded at the girl in his team and she began to work her way methodically through the drawers of the dressing table. There was a pass book for Barclays Bank, with few entries. The account showed a credit balance of just over nineteen pounds.

All the clothes in the drawers were neatly folded. Everything was clean. Blouses, sweaters, tights, underwear. A bright suntop and blue shorts, neatly pressed, reminding them that it had been summer when she disappeared. A methodical girl, this, before her abrupt departure. Or methodical parents, after it.

And in the bottom one of the three long drawers, the posters they had expected, still with the strips of sellotape which had attached them to the walls sticking to the corners. Johnson looked at the picture of a pop group with shaven heads, thrusting four pelvises at the camera, oozing a phallic aggression. He took a pace and looked at the wall. "No sign of where the posters were stuck to the plaster," he said thoughtfully.

"The master detective strikes again!" sneered Watts from the doorway. He was smiling when Johnson turned to face him. "Decorated the room last month, didn't I? Looks all the better for a lick of emulsion, don't you think, Mr Plod?" He snorted an open contempt for the futility of their actions. "Be downstairs if you want me. I'm not paid to waste public money, like some." They heard him tramp heavily, dismissively, down the stairs and throw himself into his chair in the lounge. The television sound blared up at them; then its volume was increased, as if even that could be turned into a kind of insult.

Johnson found that the young constable was looking at him to see if he was rattled. He grinned at her and shrugged. "Takes all sorts, don't it? Never stop 'em talking: they give away more about themselves than they ever learn from us." He shut the bedroom door hard, so that its closure would be registered even above the noise from the television. People, even prats like Watts, imagined all kind of things were going on when they had to use their imaginations. "Take your time over the wardrobe. Then we'll be off; the boys have almost finished downstairs."

It was a double wardrobe, occupying all of one of the narrow walls of the rectangular room. It was full of clothes: dresses, formal and informal, winter and summer; trousers and jeans; shirts, blouses and things that Johnson could identify only vaguely as 'tops'. There were at least a dozen pairs of shoes on the floor of the wardobe. The girl went through everything slowly, methodically, inspecting the labels, turning out the seams.

She seemed to work more slowly as she went along the rail, and eventually Johnson, who could see little that was unusual about the collection, said, "Come on, Rosie, there's no need to impress me with your thoroughness. If there's nothing there, let's be on our way."

"Nothing specific, sarge. But it's strange, all the same."

"What's strange? Too old for her or something, are they? Perhaps they're not all hers. We can—"

"No, it's not that, sarge. I'm sure these are exactly the kind of thing a girl like Alison would like to have. I'm a few years older, but there are things here I'd kill for myself."

"Unfortunate choice of phrase, that. Good job the sensitive

60

stepfather is safely downstairs. You mean this is good stuff?" He walked over and fingered the sleeve of a silk blouse.

"And how! There are single dresses in here that you wouldn't touch under a couple of hundred pounds. And look at the labels. Gucci, Armani. Nothing in here has come cheap. The shoes are the same. Best part of a hundred quid a pair for most of them."

Jack Johnson picked up some of the shoes, inspecting the heels. "Scarcely worn," he said, his excitement rising despite himself. "They haven't been here very long, have they?"

She shook her head. "Bought in the last year, by the look of them. The same applies to the clothes. You can tell from a fashion point of view that most of them must have been bought in the few months before she died. There's two or three thousand pounds' worth in here, I'm sure."

They took the clothes down the stairs in large polythene bags. "We're taking these things away. I'll give you a receipt for them. Do you know where they came from?" Johnson said to the clearly surprised Watts.

"No. Why should I?"

"No reason. They're expensive. Was she given them, by any chance?"

"Don't know, do I?" And wouldn't tell you if I did, his demeanour indicated.

"We shall find out, soon enough, I'm sure. It's easier with good clothes, you see, and these are very good. There aren't too many shops sell makes like these."

They left him standing worried at the front door of the house. "Perhaps the bugger's just mad he didn't sell the stuff off while he had the chance," said Johnson. But somehow he felt Robert Watts had more worries about the death of his stepdaughter than that.

Jamie Allen was a Roman Catholic. At least, he came from a Roman Catholic family. He was not sure about himself, these days. Not since Alison.

He lived in an Edwardian house, high-gabled, with most of its dark bricks covered in ivy. An eminently desirable gentleman's residence, an estate agent would have said. To Jamie it seemed dark and forbidding, particularly with twilight approaching on this October day. He was relieved to see that both of his parents were still out. He could not face his mother's quizzing about the events of the day at school, her speculation about why the police had still not interviewed him about Alison.

He opened the heavy front door with his own key; he was glad he had fought the battle to win that. Possession of your own key was part of being an adult. And he was certainly that now; in another ten days, he would be eighteen, able to vote, and to die for his country in battle. He had used that argument when he had fought for his key, and his father had smiled at him and conceded. He walked straight past the little image of Christ with the tiny glass of holy water at its base which hung from the wall near the front door. He never dipped his fingers in the water and signed himself with the cross now, as he would once have done automatically when he entered the house. What a load of bollocks all that was! Jamie enjoyed the coarse vigour of that dismissal, the slight hint of blasphemous daring that the thought gave him.

He made himself a mug of tea and took it up the stairs and along the wide landing to his own room at the end of it. He threw his case on to the armchair and lay back on his bed with his eyes closed for a moment, feeling suddenly very tired. When he had drunk his tea, he would get his books out and start making notes for his History essay. Oliver Cromwell: a fascinating figure, flawed but powerful. Not the ogre his Catholic parents had painted for him, because of his campaigns in Ireland. He was quite looking forward to the reading for the essay. But he knew he wouldn't get much done tonight. Not immediately, anyway.

He lay quietly for a moment in the darkening room, sipping his tea, trying to calm the mind which raced ahead of him with thoughts of Alison and what he would tell the police. Then he sighed, switched on the light and drew the heavy curtains across the high sash window. The big portrait of the Sacred Heart of Jesus on the wall opposite his bed seemed more oppressive than ever. It would mean a row with his mother, a big one, to get rid of it, but he would take that on, once all this business was over. She meant well, did Mum, wanted the best for him, he supposed. But she would have to be shown that he was his own man now.

Then he saw it. Saw that she had been in here again, changing things, when he had asked her not to, had thought he had secured her promise not to. And not just moving things around. Altering the most important thing of all. The photograph of himself and Alison, arms twined round each others' waists, hair blowing in the summer breeze, faces smiling breathlessly at the camera, had gone. It had been removed from its position in pride of place on the narrow mantelpiece of the metal fireplace in the corner of the room.

In its place was the cheap plaster statue of the Virgin and Child which a pious great aunt, now dead, had brought to the house from Rome when he was a small child. He had taken the crude effigy from here months ago and consigned it to the obscurity of the box room, amidst the dusty furniture and the suitcases which came out once a year for the family holiday. Now here it was back, with its cheap, sentimental smile on the face of the Madonna and its absurd two-year-old head on the shoulders of what should have been a baby. And in the place reserved for his Alison!

All Jamie's anxiety and frustration were suddenly concentrated on that ridiculous statue. It blazed at him intensely, for the ceiling spotlight he had installed himself last year was trained precisely upon this spot. He had to be rid of it, and for good. He opened the curtains, flung up the sash window. Then he seized the plaster effigy, drew back his arm as far as he could, and flung the statue far out into the darkness. He heard it shatter on the terrace below him, as he had known it would. He stood for a moment, breathing heavily, waiting for the divine retribution his upbringing still half-persuaded him should fall upon such an act.

But there was no thunderbolt, no admonitory voice from heaven. He went across to the bottom drawer where he knew it would be, drew out the silver frame with its picture of the smiling duo, and restored it to its proper position of eminence upon the mantelpiece. He smiled down at the photograph, then stooped to place his lips for a moment against the cool, unresponding glass. "Back in your place, my darling!" he murmured softly.

As if he had triggered it with this action, the phone rang in the hall below him, startling him in the empty house. He ran down the stairs, stopped for an instant to compose himself before he picked up the instrument and said, "Oldford 2910. Jamie Allen speaking."

"The very man! This is Detective Sergeant Hook, from the CID at Oldford. We need to have a word with you, Jamie. You probably know what about."

It was happening, then, at last. But at least the Sergeant had called him a man.

They didn't like you going out in the evenings, when you were at the refuge for battered women. There were no rules to say so, but the group pressures were strong. Unity is strength, they said. Don't isolate yourself, keep the team around you and you won't be in any danger.

Kate Watts waited until five minutes into *Coronation Street*, then stole softly down the stairs and through the big door. Almost all the women watched that: it was a kind of group ritual, uniting the bright and the dim in that strange place. She'd have to think of something to explain why she hadn't been there, but she could say that she'd fallen asleep on her bed. People did that often enough, making up for lost time and the disturbed domestic nights which had driven them here.

She walked into town, feeling no danger, enjoying passing men who scarcely even noticed her. She found the café easily enough. A modest enough little place, definitely a snack-bar 'caff' rather than a restaurant; not unlike the one Gail Platt ran in the soap she had just left behind. It did a brisk enough trade during the day with workers and shoppers, but it was almost empty now. A tired woman was wiping the formica table tops in a ritual which had long since become automatic, wishing away the half hour which was all that was left until closing time. Kate ordered a cup of tea she did not want and sat at the table furthest away from the window.

The girl arrived within five minutes. Hilary Jones: when Kate had seen the name on the message pad in the hostel, she had had to think hard to pin a face on that name. She bought her own tea; Kate was glad of that; she had already bought one cup she did not need, and she would need to watch her money carefully, if she was to contemplate life without Robert. As the girl carried the cup to the table and sat down opposite her, Kate thought sadly that she was the very opposite of her Alison. Squat where Alison had been willowy-tall, spotty with acne where Alison's skin had been so smooth and soft, greasy-haired where Alison's golden waves had fallen soft and shining at the sides of her head.

Not attractive to men, presumably. Perhaps a good thing too, Kate thought sourly. Look where beauty had got her. Look where it had got poor Alison. Suddenly she resented this plain, earnest girl, just for being alive.

"I got your message," Kate said roughly. "How'd you know where I was?"

"The old lady told me. The one who lives on the corner of your road."

"I see. Nosy old cow, she is."

"She means well, I think. She asked me to give you her love, if I saw you." The girl was taken aback by this aggression. She had sent her message only because she thought she had better give her information to Alison's mother, rather than to the police. She had said scarcely anything earlier in the day, when she had sat with the rest of the group and those two big detectives in Mrs Peplow's room, because she had thought she must speak to Allie's mum first. Hilary picked up her spoon and stirred vigorously at her tea, even though there was no sugar in it. The woman behind the distant counter folded her arms and looked at them with a sigh, willing them to finish their business and get on their way.

Hilary said, "The police saw us today, asking us for anything we could tell them about Alison. I didn't say anything. But there is something. Perhaps nothing to do with her death. Probably. I just thought I should tell it to you, not them." Her speech was becoming more and more staccato. She looked as if she was going to cry. Kate reached a hand across the table and put it on top of the chubby fist which still held the spoon. "All right, m'dear. I didn't mean to seem abrupt. You tell me about it."

The kindness made the tears brim over in relief, so that for a moment the girl could not speak. Kate remembered Hilary clearly enough now. She lived within a hundred yards of the Watts; her family had moved there four years ago from Swansea. She had gone to and from the school with Alison, had remained a close friend of her lively daughter, though always in her shadow. The kind of girl who was never a threat and always a support. The kind of companion a girl might choose for a confidante. And Alison had done just that, it seemed.

The things Hilary told Kate now could only have been told by a confidante, could only have been kept secret until now by such a one. She told her tale haltingly, between little sobs and huge, uneven intakes of breath, with the Welsh accent she thought she had lost coming through with the emotion. It was an awful thing she had to tell, and the horror of it sprung more vividly before her as she fought for the words and watched the revulsion stealing across the face between the whitening fists on the other side of the table. She got it out at last, completed the story, or all she could tell of it, answered the bludgeoning questions which came out of the face. She said, trying to signify the end of it, "I did right, didn't I, to come to you?"

Reeling from the news, Kate could not give the frightened, exhausted girl the reassurance she wanted. She said harshly, "How can you be sure of this? You can't go around spreading things like this, you silly girl!"

The tears ran free and unchecked now down poor Hilary's acned cheeks. "It's true, Mrs Watts. Honestly it is. Alison told it all to me herself. Just as I've told it to you. I haven't added anything, really I haven't. I – I just thought you should know. In case – in case he might have killed her!" The nightmare had been put into words. She buried her face in an already sodden handkerchief.

Kate said something to comfort her, some vague words to reassure her that she had done the right thing. They went out together, past the curious woman at the counter, into the cool night and the first drizzle of rain. Kate had just enough presence of mind to call after the girl, "Don't tell anyone else, Hilary, will you? Keep it to yourself, for God's sake!"

Though what God could have to do with such awful things she could not begin to imagine.

Chapter Nine

AS they went up the wide stone steps of the Edwardian house, they could hear raised voices, even through the heavy oak door. And Lambert could see as soon as it was opened that they had come at a bad time.

"Mrs Allen? We're here to see your son, Jamie."

"So I understand. It really is most inconvenient that you should come to our house at night like this." There were spots of high colour at the top of her cheeks. She was erect and proud, a tall woman who was used to having her own way. She had little or no make-up and her greying hair was bunched high on her head. She wore a sage-green cardigan over a paisley dress. Bert Hook, who had been brought up in a Barnardo's home and thought himself an expert on severe, middle-class women, thought that she probably had pious tendencies and that she went well with this gloomy, ill-lit house. A throw-back, perhaps, to a more authoritarian age. He did not envy Jamie Allen.

The boy came into the hall and stood behind his mother. Lambert smiled, trying to remove some of the tension that had been building in the house when these official visitors arrived. "We can do this down at the station if you think it more appropriate, Mrs Allen. We agreed with your son that we should come here."

"It's all right, Mother, really it is. Sergeant Hook explained that they thought it would be less embarrassing for me to see them here rather than at the school during the day, and I agreed with him."

His mother's lips tightened at this assertion of independence. "That's true enough, anyway. You've drawn quite enough attention to yourself over that girl as it is, without having the whole

school sniggering about it and thinking you've been arrested."
She turned back to Lambert. "We'll go into the drawing room.
You can say whatever you have to say in there. And that will
be an end of it."

"We shall decide that, Mrs Allen. We may or may not need to
see Jamie again. That will depend both on how frank he is with
us and on what we subsequently find from other people. We are
still at an early stage of our investigation. And I really think we
need to see Jamie on his own."

He thought for a moment she was going to erupt; he had not
met such patrician hostility at close quarters for a long time. But
she controlled herself and said between teeth that were almost
closed, "That is not going to happen. Jamie is still a juvenile, not
yet eighteen. He has the right to be accompanied by a responsible
adult at any interview. I am asserting that right, Inspector."

Amused to find himself summarily demoted, Lambert said,
"I'm afraid that isn't so, madam. This isn't a formal interview,
in any case: we're hoping Jamie is going to assist us with our
enquiries, as any responsible citizen should. But we don't need
an adult present when interviewing someone over sixteen."

Jamie's flushed face brightened and he came forward. "I told you
that, Mother. And I'm perfectly capable of looking after myself.
Why don't we do this in my room upstairs, Mr Lambert?"

His mother's face hardened, the lips setting in a thin line. "There
isn't room in there. And it won't be tidy, if I know you." There
was something further, a vague sense of impropriety which she
could not voice. She wanted to say that a bedroom was a wholly
unsuitable, even a shocking place in which to take strangers, even
of the same sex. But she had no idea how to voice that thought,
had not even formulated it properly for herself.

Jamie said, "It's all right. The room's plenty big enough for
three. I'll bring a couple of extra stand chairs in from the box
room." And before she could object, he bustled away up the wide
staircase, leaving them staring after him from the hall.

His mother raised her hand, then slapped it against her hip
in frustration as he disappeared. "Come in here for a moment,
please," she said imperiously and turned away from them into
the drawing room where she had wanted them to conduct the

68

interview. Lambert exchanged a meaningful look with Hook, then led his sergeant into the room. It was a surprisingly cheerful room, with the flames of a real fire blinking at them from a big marble fireplace on the long wall and glasses glinting reflections from the china cabinet in the corner. The high ceiling was almost invisible, for the light in the room came from a standard lamp and two table lamps. She turned to face them and said, "My son had nothing to do with this death, you know. He can't tell you anything which can be of any relevance." Patiently, firmly, Lambert reiterated the formula he had gone through with so many people over the years. "We shall have to decide that for ourselves, Mrs Allen, in due course. What we have to do at the moment is to build up as full a picture as we can of the murder victim. Someone who knew her as well as Jamie can clearly help us to do that."

"He didn't know her that well, you know. Don't let anyone persuade you that he did. Not even him."

Sometimes people's denials were more interesting than the information they offered. Lambert said, "I see. How did you see his relationship with Miss Watts, Mrs Allen?"

Her face relaxed a little, for the first time. She was going to be allowed to say her piece about the girl, after all. It might even be better without her son present; she could be more trenchant about the little slut. But she had better be quick about it. "Jamie was infatuated with her, for a little while, that's all. She was older than him. And – and more experienced. That girl had boys round her like flies round a honeypot." The sibilants hissed as her face registered her distaste at the thought. She looked as if her mouth had suddenly filled with vinegar.

Hook said, "Alison was ten months older than your son, to be precise. But you think that she took advantage of him in some way?"

She looked at Bert as if he was something dubious the cat had brought in and dropped on the rich Persian carpet. "You need to understand about Jamie, Sergeant. He's a brilliant boy. The best in his year. Perhaps the best they've ever had. He'll be going to Cambridge, in due course."

Lambert said, "The school certainly gave us to understand that your son was an intelligent young man. They expect him to get good results at A level."

Mrs Allen's smile could have patronised for England. It said more plainly than words that this dubious educational establishment was lucky to have her son, that he would bring it more honour than it could ever offer to him. "James has been outstanding throughout his school career. He is our only son, Inspector Lambert, and a sensitive boy. He has been brought up in a strong religion, given strong convictions." She glanced nervously at the door and dropped her voice a little. "Until – until this girl came upon the scene, his father and I even entertained the idea that he might enter the priesthood, in due course. Not that we ever put any pressure upon him in that respect, of course."

Not half, thought Bert Hook. Wiping all expression save a puzzled smile from his face, he said, "So Alison Watts was Jamie's first girlfriend, Mrs Allen?"

She winced at the expression, as visibly as if he had suggested her son was on some sort of rake's progress into depravity. "James had associated easily enough with girls, Sergeant, from the time he first went to school. The Catholic primary school is mixed, of course. Unfortunately, the only single sex Catholic Grammar school in Gloucestershire has now closed. We had to let James go to our local comprehensive and mix with all sorts of beliefs, but he handled it well. Very well, until this – this young trollop came along."

It was a word neither of them had heard for years, and it was plainly the worst expression this daughter of the Church could bring herself to utter. Hook bit his lip, concentrated fiercely upon the intricate design of the carpet at his feet, and resolved to let Lambert do the talking. The Superintendent, deliberately casual, almost insulting, said, "Bad influence, was she, Alison Watts?"

"The very worst, Inspector. I don't like to speak ill of the dead." Her lips pressed together twice, proclaiming that she was very definitely going to do just that. "But she was a Jezebel, that girl!"

Lambert suddenly felt that he had had enough of this stifling house and its matriarch. "It takes two to tango, Mrs Allen. So they say."

70

Her neck arched slowly backwards, making her considerable height seem even greater. "If by that you mean that two people are involved in a relationship, that is obviously so. Hardly worth stating, I should have thought. But there is no doubt in my mind who took the initiative in this – this particular coupling!"

She stopped, aghast at her use of the word, aware of its sexual connotations from the days when she too had studied literature. She had not meant to use it, had intended something else entirely, but it had sprung unbidden to her lips from that dreadful image of her pure son writhing in naked carnality with that awful, shameless girl. She tried desperately to lower the tone of this for these strangers who were intruding upon her most intimate sufferings. "They met at school, of course. They were studying the same subjects. Jamie no doubt began by helping her with her work – he's always been generous like that. But I've no doubt that she set her cap at him, that—"

"You've no doubt because that's what you want to think! You make it up as you would like it to have happened!"

Jamie Allen stood in the doorway, quivering, red-faced, scarcely able to control himself in his anger. He had opened the heavy door without a sound, making them wonder how long he had stood on the other side of it, how much of this he had heard before he intervened. Most of it, Hook surmised: when you were seventeen and stumbling towards adulthood, you were perpetually curious to know what the rest of the world thought of you.

Jamie stood for a long moment, breathing heavily, savouring the shock his entry had brought to his mother. Then he controlled himself, turned to the CID men he had scarcely registered in the fury of his arrival, and said, "If you would like to come upstairs to my room, please, I'll tell you everything you want to know about Alison and me."

He led them through the high, wide hall and up on to the landing. The lighting was poor: a 60 watt bulb in each of these large areas, Hook thought. It seemed appropriately dim and gloomy for this oppressive house. It made the boy's own room seem like a cavern of white light. He had installed three ceiling spotlights; the walls were light and the yellow velvet curtains were the lightest shade they had seen in the house. A tiny fan heater hummed beneath the

71

table, which had open books upon its surface; the high-ceilinged room was pleasantly warm. There were pictures on the walls: a family grouping, with a young Jamie in short trousers sitting cross-legged at the front amidst a dozen adults, a picture of Jamie at about twelve in tennis clothes, beside a man who had dropped a protective hand on his shoulder, presumably the father they had not yet seen. And in pride of place on the narrow mantelpiece of the old fireplace, picked out by one of the spotlights, a picture of Jamie with Alison Watts, both of them looking very young and carefree, sitting on the grass with arms loosely around each other's waists.

Lambert was amused by the seating arrangements the boy had set up for them. He had dragged in a second comfortable armchair and set it alongside his own. He now seated the two interrogators in these and sat himself awkwardly on the stand chair, which he turned round from the table to face them. It left him slightly elevated, and in another context they would have known that the subject was trying to maintain the position of physical eminence in the group. Here it was no more than a natural politeness: Jamie was affording the more comfortable chairs to his elders and betters, as the upbringing he now affected to despise had taught him to do. He went to the door of the room and looked out on to the landing before he closed it carefully; the action made them more than ever convinced that he had listened to the bulk of their exchanges with his mother downstairs.

Lambert said briskly, "There's no reason why this should take very long, if you are frank with us, Mr Allen."

The boy blushed immediately: he was not used to being addressed as an adult. Lambert found himself wondering how successfully he would handle a Cambridge University interview. Jamie said, "I think I knew Allie better than anyone else you will have seen."

It was the arrogance of youth, of course, asserting that his relationship was more important even than that of parents. Jamie was even a little annoyed at the suggestion that his account of the girl would not take long, thought Hook, as if that somehow diminished the intensity of what had gone between them. Lambert said calmly, "I take it that the two of you were lovers?"

72

"In every sense of the word." Jamie spoke defiantly, with an involuntary glance at the door he had shut so carefully.

He obviously expected that this open assertion would cause some sort of sensation. He looked almost disappointed when Lambert said calmly, "And when did this relationship begin?" and Hook prepared to record the details in his notebook.

"We've known each other for a long time, of course. Since we first went to Oldford Comprehensive. But we weren't in the same form then. We first got together when we were studying for GCSEs. And it was in the summer holidays, whilst we were getting ready to begin our A levels in the sixth form, that – that the relationship deepened and we became very close."

Lambert looked into the flushed, animated young face. "You mean that that is when you first went to bed together?"

"Yes. I suppose so. Except that the first time was outdoors, under a summer sky and white clouds, with the leaves rustling high above us." He looked for a reaction to this picture, which he had obviously re-run many times, but received nothing more than a curt nod. "What I meant was that it was at that time that we fell in love – what we felt for each other went much deeper than mere sex." He was enough a child of his upbringing to assert that sex was merely incidental, when both of them could see how important it had been to him.

Lambert wondered what the dead girl would have said to this. Would she have seen the relationship as this intelligent but desperately callow young man was so determined to see it? The familiar regret that murder was the one crime in which you could not take the victim's view made him sigh with quiet frustration. "We deal with facts, Jamie. You're telling us that you first had sex with Alison about fifteen months ago."

"Fifteen months and nine days ago, actually." He blushed, not at the recollection, but because he realised how this precision exposed the intensity of his feelings. He was an acute young man, for all his naivety and the raw vulnerability of his emotions.

Lambert stood up, walked to the mantelpiece, picked up the photograph of Jamie Allen and Alison Watts from its position of honour in the spotlight, studied that carefree outdoor scene with the two happy, unguarded faces and the wind ruffling their hair for ever. He smiled down at the upturned adolescent face which watched him so closely. "This was taken last summer, I suppose?"

"Yes. At the end of August. Just before we went into the sixth form." He glanced again at the shut door, said, almost furtively, "I let the *Gazette* borrow the negative of that. They want to print a picture of Alison, to help you in the hunt. Mum won't be pleased when she sees it on the front page!" He smiled with grim satisfaction.

Lambert smiled too, but that was at the idea that the bumbling local rag might help them in their hunt for the killer of this now long dead girl. He said, "But the relationship had cooled, hadn't it, Jamie, in the months before Alison disappeared?" He watched denial spring into the boy's face, held up his hand quickly. "Be as honest as possible, please, Jamie. I'm sure you are as anxious as we are to find out who has done this awful thing to Alison."

The boy nodded, his narrow shoulders drooping beneath his sweatshirt. He had defied his mother, asserted his love for Allie, been listened to by the police when he had thought he might be reviled. But now it was time to admit what he would rather have denied: he could see that, when this man who seemed to him too old and wise to be a policeman put the matter so starkly to him. Obviously he had to let them know how much he wanted Allie's killer to be caught. Jamie said softly, with infinite regret, "We weren't as close as we had been, in the weeks before Allie went, no. But that was a temporary thing. We'd have been all right again, if – if she'd only been given time to see—"

His voice tailed away, and it seemed for a moment as if he would weep. Lambert said, "To see what, Jamie? There were other men in her life, as well as you, weren't there?"

"Who told you that?" His flaring anger banished the tears which had threatened.

"We talk to a lot of people, Jamie, in a murder enquiry. And our first task is to build up a picture of the victim and her last movements. We treat what people tell us as confidential. Just as we shall treat whatever you have to tell us about Alison and her friends as confidential."

"Friends! They were no friends of hers, the ones who came

between us. Not real friends, anyway. This would never have happened, without them!"

"Tell us about them, Jamie." This was Bert Hook, calmly persuasive as usual with the young, looking up with an encouraging smile over the top of his notebook.

"I can't!"

"This isn't the moment to hold anything back, Jamie. If there is anything at all you can tell us about anyone close to Alison, you must—"

"I don't mean I won't. I can't. I don't know who they are!"

It was wrung from him like a cry of pain. It was agony for him to admit that there were people who had been closer to this girl he loved in her last days than he had. Lambert watched the anguished twistings of the young face for a moment before he said, "Were the people you're so concerned about in Oldford?"

"No. I don't know." He ran both hands suddenly through his thick black hair. "Oh, it's true, I didn't see as much of Allie in those last weeks. We'd have been all right, given a bit of time, I'm sure. But pretty girls have a lot of attention, and sometimes it turns their heads a bit."

Other men, then. The CID men had known that, all along. Perhaps Jamie Allen was having to admit it to himself for the first time. "Indeed it does. So who were these other men, Jamie?"

"I don't know. She – she went off somewhere. On Friday nights." He looked down at his feet, twisted the toes a little, experimentally, like a small child discovering his extremities for the first time and finding them of absorbing interest.

"Every Friday night, Jamie?"

"Yes, in those last months. Sometimes she went off at weekends as well, but every Friday." His face contorted with misery at the memory of it and the arguments it had caused between them.

"And where did she go on those Friday nights, Jamie?" Lambert's steady, unemotional voice drew him on like a hypnotist's.

But it was no good. Jamie said wretchedly, "I don't know. She wouldn't tell me. Threatened to finish with me altogether, when I pressed it."

And that would have been only a matter of time, in any case, thought Lambert sadly. Age and experience removed the ridiculous

75

illusions of youth, but sometimes life was more pleasant with a few illusions. He said, "You've no idea where she might have gone on these occasions? Or who might have been with her?"

"No. She wouldn't tell me. It was out of Oldford, anyway. And not with anyone I know. I'd have found out, if it had been."

He would, too, thought Lambert. A determined young man, this, though it was probably better for him that he had been left in ignorance. But not for them. There were enough avenues for them to explore in this damned case, without bringing in sinister unidentified males to add to the possibilities.

Hook, accepting a nod from his chief, said, "When did you last see Alison, Jamie?"

He reddened at the question, though he had expected it, had rehearsed his answer to it. It meant he was a suspect, that they were checking when he had last been close to his lovely, slaughtered Allie. "I saw her at school on the Friday morning. At morning break: eleven o'clock. We broke up for the summer holidays at lunch time on that last Friday. July the twenty-third."

It was as precise as he had been earlier. Yet somehow this assertion did not carry quite the same ringing truth. He was still staring at his feet, which had ceased to move now. Hook studied the intense face for a moment, then wrote down the time. "And you didn't see Alison Watts again after eleven o'clock on that Friday?"

"No."

Lambert said quietly, "Your relationship with Alison Watts cooled over those last months, Jamie. You must have had arguments over that. Did you kill her?"

"No! I loved her!" The words came in a desperate shout.

"That doesn't mean you didn't kill her, Jamie. We often see love turn into murderous hatred in this job, I'm afraid."

The boy looked up at him, for the first time in minutes. "*Je l'ai trop aimé pour ne le point haïr,*" he quoted with a grim nod.

"Racine. *Andromaque*, isn't it?" He grinned at the boy's look of astonishment. " 'I have loved him too much not to feel hate for him.' I did French for A level as well, you see. A long time ago. But I'm often reminded of that quotation when we see passion turning into violence in our CID work."

"Yes, I see. But I didn't hate Allie. We'd have got back together all right, if we'd been given time."

"All right. Have you any idea at all who might have killed her, then?"

"No. I've thought about it often enough, God knows. But I haven't come up with anyone."

Lambert stood up. "If you have any further thoughts on the matter, please get in touch with us right away. You needn't fear that any innocent person will suffer. Contrary to the opinion of a lot of your contemporaries, we don't just want a conviction at any price."

A few minutes after they had gone, Jamie left his bright warm room and went down the gloomy staircase. His mother's heart contracted when she saw how drained he looked. She wanted to go and throw her arms round him. But because the human mind is a strange instrument, she did no such thing. She looked instead for some way to assert herself, to repay him for the hurt he had done to her in front of strangers twenty minutes earlier.

"Did you tell them about your final meeting with that girl? About the row you had on that last Friday night?" she said waspishly.

Cheltenham is one of the finest spa towns in Europe. It has a wealth of Regency houses, bordering squares, crescents, terraces and open spaces. The wide streets and tree-shaded open spaces which form the basis of its late-Georgian elegance were laid out early in the nineteenth century. Senior service personnel and professional men still find this a good place to retire. The town remains the symbol of conservative England in respectable retirement.

Nevertheless, Cheltenham is also what its publicity officers like to call 'a lively modern community'. It is now virtually the same size as its more ancient neighbour, Gloucester, and it has the problems as well as the vibrancy of a modern industrial town. It has its modern industries as well as its festivals and spacious squares. And it has inevitably its share of serious crime, and of the villains who direct it.

On that October Friday night, whilst Lambert and Hook were talking to Jamie Allen, a man sat alone in an office at the back of a

Cheltenham night club. He was a thick-set man of fifty, with huge shoulders and bushy black eyebrows beneath a thick crop of curly hair. He had a small scar on the right of his forehead, where a knife had narrowly missed his eye twenty years earlier, He was studying a copy of the very *Gazette* to which young Jamie Allen had been so willing to give his favourite picture of Alison Watts.

The picture was reproduced on the front page, as the young man had hoped, but Mrs Allen would not after all be scandalised by the sight of her son with his arm round the girl. Jamie had been cut out of the picture, and a blown-up version of the dead girl's head and shoulders was all that was shown. The enlargement and the newsprint reproduction had made the focus less sharp, but Alison's laughing face looked even younger and more attractive in this form.

'BRUTAL MURDER OF THE LAUGHING GIRL' ran the headline, and the copy below made play with 'the ancient market town of Oldford' where Alison had lived out her short life until she was 'strangled by person or persons unknown'. After a purple passage explaining how 'the picturesque Wye had held its grisly burden' for so many weeks before it surrendered it, there was a short account of Superintendent Lambert and a list of his earlier murder cases, which had made him something of a local celebrity. The reporter ended by risking the thought that even 'the formidable Jack Lambert' was baffled by the case at this opening stage of his investigation.

The thick-set man knew John Lambert, as he knew most of the senior policemen in the area. He respected the Superintendent: he had learned a long time ago not to underestimate his opponents. His name was Eddie Hurst, and as crime had spread its tentacles through the developing town, he had grown fat upon it. He had a finger in most of the poisonous pies that fed the criminal fraternity, and he directed several of the more lucrative enterprises. He ran two legitimate if sleazy night clubs, and used this façade to hide his more profitable interests in porn, drugs and robbery with violence. He had done time, but that was for minor offences, and many years ago now. You didn't do porridge when you were big time.

But you had to make sure they couldn't tie you in with things like this.

Hurst scanned the sparse facts which the reporter had tried his best to expand into a story, glanced again at the picture of the smiling girl which spread over four columns above it. She looked more innocent than he remembered her – more innocent than he knew for a fact she was. Had been, rather: silly young cow. He cursed softly, automatically, mouthing his opinion of 'fucking headmasters' who complicated his world. There was in fact only one such irritant. He looked up the number, not in the directory, but on a single sheet that he drew from a drawer in his desk.

Then he dialled the home of Thomas Murray, MA, FRSA.

Chapter Ten

SATURDAY provided them with a perfect morning. There was not a cloud to be seen; the sun cleared away the wisps of autumn mist from the still Cotswold valleys, then shone unblinkingly down over a population staring sleepily at the weekend.

"The kind of autumn morning people fly to Portugal for," said Lambert cheerfully as they drove along the deserted lanes. Hook grunted what was probably agreement. He did not approve of early morning buoyancy; moreover, he had heard this thought from his chief before. And the morning was not so fresh and new for him: with his two boisterous sons still blissfully asleep, Bert had spent two hours with his Open University studies before a hurried breakfast. "We're no nearer to solving this one," he reminded his chief sourly.

"But there are lies flying about," said Lambert gnomically. "And lies are always interesting to master detectives like us, aren't they? The question is, which lies are the important ones?" He smiled happily at a group of sheep clustered behind a gate and volunteered no further guidance as to the way his convoluted mind was working. Hook glowered at the autumn glory of the trees and refused to be drawn into further questioning. They would be at the school in a minute.

Oldford Comprehensive was a very different place at nine o'clock on a Saturday morning than on other days of the week. There was even time and space to notice the rich mahogany leaves of the lines of ornamental trees as they drove up the drive which on the five previous days had been thronged with noisy children at this time. There was no other car in the car park to the left of the school's main entrance. Even the teams for the Saturday morning games had not yet arrived.

The caretaker introduced himself fully. Like many others involved for the first and last time in a murder enquiry, he wished to prolong his contact with melodrama; death has an eerie glamour which no other crime carries. "George Phillips. Caretaker. Resident on the site. My name used to be on the board at the gates, until this bugger came." He twitched his head at the office above him, then glanced automatically over his shoulder, to make sure that 'this bugger', who was obviously Thomas Murray, Headmaster, was not within earshot.

He led them into the deserted reception area of the school, through an assembly hall which looked even larger for being empty, and down a staircase to the capacious basement area of the school buildings. On this journey, he wheezed an unbroken monologue of complaint, beginning with the coke boilers and manual loadings of the 'fifties, which had apparently given him his bronchitis as a young man, and proceeding to a catalogue of the disciplinary shortcomings of modern education. "The lads give you lip as soon as look at you, and the girls wear skirts up round their bottoms." Phillips leered horribly at the ceiling on this last thought, convincing them that he could be persuaded of the desirability of this single educational reform. As if bringing the ship of discipline safely into harbour, he concluded with, "And nowadays even the bloody teachers dress as if they was going to work in the garden!"

With this crushing final demonstration of the decadence of civilisation at the millennium, they stood before the long rank of steel lockers which was the purpose of their visit. " 'ardly worth while for two bigwigs like you, this is, you know," said the caretaker confidentially, as if he hoped that his advice might save public money in the future. Lambert did not tell him that he had come here on a Saturday because he wanted to get a feel of this place without people around, without exciting the attention of children who were already full of febrile imaginings about their peers and the staff. "Open it, please," he said curtly.

Phillips produced a large bunch of keys from the capacious front pocket of his overalls. He selected the smallest one and announced that it was the skeleton key for the lockers in front of them, as if he hoped to assert a position of trust from the fact that

81

he held it. "This is Alison Watts's locker. Number thirty-seven. But you won't find nothing."

"And why are you so sure of that, Mr Phillips?" said Hook, as their guide struggled to find the right angle for the key in the gloom of the basement half-light.

"Been through it before, 'aven't we?"

"When was this?"

"Weeks ago. During the summer holidays."

Of course. When Alison Watts was first reported as a MISPA, some constable would have gone through the locker with a member of staff, searching dutifully for any clue as to the whereabouts of the missing girl. Hook said heavily, "And what did you find then, Mr Phillips?"

The caretaker shrugged, struggling still to turn this smallest of his bunch of keys in the lock. "Books. Bugger all else." He grunted his relief as the long green metal door swung open at last before them. The tall, coffin-like space was empty. A thin coating of dust had penetrated through the ventilator slits in the door. No books. No photographs. No letters. No sign of the diary so beloved of fiction.

There was a shelf at the top of the tall locker, where one might have expected to find a hat or a scarf, or even some small, significant personal belonging. But here too there was nothing to be seen. A smaller man would have had to feel the surface to be certain of that, but from his height of six feet three, Lambert could see the surface of the metal shelf as others would not have. He almost forebore to reach into the locker, because even in the near darkness of the basement he could see that it was empty. It must have been some long-forgotten thoroughness from his early days as a city constable, or some sense of desperation at arriving here so long after events, that made him reach a lean hand into the recesses of the locker. He felt without hope around its cold green metal.

Nothing, as he had expected. Then, as he was about to withdraw his hand, his middle finger touched something, felt it catch momentarily beneath the nail. He felt again, scratching with his finger tips at the topmost corner of the dark rectangle. Then he drew forth a tiny scrap of paper, grey with dust and ragged on two of its edges, where it had been torn from the corner of an exercise book or note pad. One side of it was blank. The other contained eleven figures in a neat, round hand. Five digits, then a gap, then six more. A phone number. He glanced at the first section of numbers: 01452. "The Gloucester code," he muttered to Hook.

The sergeant slipped the fragment into his notebook before the widening eyes of George Phillips. It would be checked out within the hour, once they were away from the caretaker's curious scrutiny. They asked him for form's sake if he could tell them anything of interest about the dead girl and her associates, though they knew he would have volunteered such information long before now if he had held it. They were almost off the premises, standing outside the caretaker's house near the gates, when Lambert said, "Mr Phillips, you said that there were books and perhaps other possessions in the locker when you opened it originally. Who was it who ordered that they should be cleared? Can you remember?"

George could, and he was eager to volunteer the information; the man was no friend of his. He was wheezing a little, for the policemen had made him move faster than was his wont. But he said promptly and delightedly, "That was the headmaster, Mr Murray. He took the things away himself."

It was five miles to the house of Jason Bullimore. They were silent for most of the journey, which suited Hook. Eventually Lambert said, "Give me the SP on this bloke again, Bert," and the Sergeant flicked to the meagre details he had already assembled in his notebook. That solid and traditional artefact was threatened occasionally with replacement by a laptop computer, but the cost had so far saved DS Hook from anything so radical.

"Mr Jason Bullimore, MA. Oxon. Aged twenty-nine. Unmarried. Head of English Department at Oldford Comprehensive. Single, but not gay, as far as we know. Probably with an eye for the girls, indeed, though in the context of his present post at Oldford that so far is little more than hearsay." Scarcely even that, thought Lambert. More the odd meaningful look, the occasional exchange of glances between staff or pupils at the school. But looks could convey more information than words, sometimes.

Bullimore's house was only just off the bus route to Hereford, but tucked away at the end of a short cul-de-sac. The seclusion was emphasised by a high hedge of leylandii at the front boundary, eight feet high, neatly clipped but uncompromisingly thick. It meant that the small detached house was only visible when one reached the gate. It was a regularly shaped, 1930s house, with a little moss on the red tiles of the roof. Square windows on each side of the oak front door made it look as if the face of the house was peering myopically at those who ventured to disturb its seclusion. There was a rectangular patch of lawn surrounded by straight borders in front of the door; the summer bedding plants had already been cleared. The neatly hoed, plantless borders seemed even on this bright autumn morning to be anticipating the winter to come.

It did not look like the house of a youngish bachelor. Such men were not usually neat gardeners who worked in advance of the seasons, in Bert Hook's now considerable experience. He was not surprised when a woman opened the door to them. "Sergeant Hook and Superintendent Lambert," he said, as they felt hastily for the warrant cards they had not expected to need. "I rang last night and arranged for us to see Mr Bullimore. I'm afraid we're a little early, but perhaps—"

"Twenty minutes early." The woman surveyed them calmly for a moment from beneath broad black eyebrows. She was tall without being willowy, busty without being voluptuous. She looked as if she were in her middle thirties, but the severity of her expression perhaps made her look a little older than she was. The doorstep gave her perhaps six inches of height, but she looked straight into Lambert's grey eyes and down upon Hook's blue ones. She sighed softly, then said, "Jason is out at present: no doubt he will be back at the time you arranged. You'd better come in."

She led them through a hall and into a sitting room that was as neat and functional as the grounds they had left outside. She gestured towards two upright armchairs. As they sat down, she said, almost as an afterthought, "I'm Mr Bullimore's sister. Barbara Bullimore. We live in this house together."

It was a curiously old-fashioned use of a young man's formal title. Perhaps she was keeping them at a distance; they had decided already that this woman probably kept most people at a distance. Despite the sibling relationship, she seemed an unlikely companion for a philanderer to share with, if that was indeed what Bullimore proved to be. Hook was intimidated, despite himself. She reminded him a little of Mrs Squeers in *Nicholas Nickleby*, but it was the association with the formidable matrons of his boyhood in a Barnardo's home rather than any literary connection which impeded him. He said unwisely, "You keep house for your brother, do you, Miss Bullimore?"

"Indeed I don't. Those days of female subservience are long gone, I'm happy to say, Sergeant." She made his rank sound like an obscenity. "I am employed full-time in the Gloucestershire Library Service. My brother and I each have our own careers, you see."

In Lambert's experience, there were two sorts of librarians: the ones who saw their mission as providing you with free access to the books you wanted, and the ones who thought it their duty to protect their precious volumes from the public at any price. Ms Bullimore was probably one of the latter. He had been happy to come here early because he knew that a premature arrival often threw a suspect a little off balance; now it seemed like a mistake.

Barbara Bullimore stood for a moment on the rug in front of the empty fireplace after they had sat down, as if she were reluctant to abandon this position of dominance. Then she pulled a stand chair from the wall and set it precisely opposite them before placing her formidable backside carefully upon it. She was a big woman, not fat, but with broad shoulders and hands. Her forearms looked very strong as she smoothed her tweed skirt unnecessarily over sturdy thighs. Perhaps lifting piles of books gave you arms like that, thought Bert Hook apprehensively. Those forearms cast him back again to the days of his youth, when house-mothers ruled with rods of iron and corporal punishment had not yet been outlawed from homes for noisy boys.

"My brother had nothing to do with the death of this wretched girl, you know," said the librarian.

85

Lambert allowed his experienced eyebrows to lift the merest fraction. "You knew Alison Watts, Miss Bullimore?"

"No. No, of course I didn't. Why should you think that?"

"Your attitude seems a little – well, a little uncharitable, if you had no reason to think ill of the girl."

The large face opposite them reddened, though whether with anger or embarrassment it was impossible to say. "Perhaps you are right to pick me up on that. I know it is conventional that one does not speak ill of the dead. But what I have read of her has given me no very high opinion of this girl. One learns when one is used to studying book reviews to read between the lines, you see." She managed a tiny, frosty smile; irony was perhaps the nearest approach to humour which this severe woman allowed herself.

Lambert reflected that she must have read copiously between the lines on this occasion. Alison Watts had been remarkably pretty, and the press's response to the waste of attractive young life had been predictably adulatory. A young angel had been brutally removed from the world, according to the columns beneath the photographs. This woman must have discussed the girl at length with her brother, or had known Alison Watts herself in some way; her reaction had been prompt and definite. She seemed now to realise that herself. "I didn't know the girl myself, of course, but she seems to have been typical of her generation in many ways, and that is no recommendation to me."

Barbara Bullimore folded her arms and looked the Superintendent in the eye, challenging him to dispute her assessment of the case. Instead, it was mild Bert Hook who took her up, perhaps unconsciously seeking revenge on the dozens of Barbara Bullimores he encountered thirty years ago when he went back to the home with his school day concluded. "You have very decided opinions about the way this young lady lived, Miss Bullimore. How much do you know about the way she died?"

She turned her attention to him calmly, weighing him as a foe before she spoke. "Nothing. Nothing, that is, beyond what I have read in the papers. I read that she was strangled with some sort of ligature and put in the River Wye, that her body remained in the river for some weeks before it was discovered. Down at Chepstow,

I believe." She was as calm and precise in her disapproval as if she had been correcting some scatterbrained borrower at her library counter. You wouldn't willingly face a fine from this formidable guardian of literature.

Yet Bert persisted. It was the kind of yeoman courage that won us two world wars, thought John Lambert beside him. "You say you read between the lines about the girl's life, Miss Bullimore. Presumably in reading about her death you have exercised the same skills. What conclusions have you formed about who might have killed her?"

Lambert expected her either to explode with wrath or to dismiss Bert's question with contemptuous disdain. Barbara Bullimore did neither. She looked at him for a moment which seemed to stretch into minutes, then said, "She was killed by a man, I should think, wouldn't you? Either by someone who had been involved in a sexual relationship with her – and I expect you already have several possibilities there – or by some random acquaintance that she met on that Friday night. I am assuming, you see, that she was killed almost immediately after she disappeared from the community. That seems a reasonable presumption to me. I should say that the likeliest thing is that she was killed after some random meeting with a stranger." For the first time since they had met her, she gave a broad and genuine smile as a thought struck her. "If I'm right, that wouldn't make things very easy for you, would it?"

"Indeed it wouldn't," agreed Lambert. "But random killings are much less common than the public thinks. Statistically the overwhelming probability is that Alison Watts was murdered by someone who had known her for some time."

"And that is why you're here today. Well, you're wasting your time, Superintendent. Jason didn't kill that girl."

"But he knew her, Miss Bullimore. For a considerable period. And taught her, latterly. He may be able to tell us things which will help us. Things about her habits and her friends. Things about her personality, perhaps, the kind of girl she was."

She sniffed. "He didn't know her well. He only came to the school three years ago, you know."

It was a curious fact to assert. In this context, three years was a long time. She seemed to be trying and failing to distance her brother from the dead girl. Interesting. But before they could pursue it, they heard the front door open and shut and footsteps move swiftly across the hall.

The young man who came into the room would never have been taken for the brother of the formidable female who had confronted them over the previous minutes. He was much more slightly built, with an open face and a ready smile which sprang to his face as he greeted them now. His light brown hair was short and neatly cut, with an attractive curl at the front which strayed a little over the right of his forehead. His blue eyes were watchful, but not hostile. They knew his age was twenty-nine, but otherwise they would have put him in his middle twenties, perhaps because his face had retained a boyish enthusiasm. They knew better than to trust appearances, but years of CID work had trained them to assess the impact of appearance on others. Their first thought was the same: here was a man who might easily have turned the head of an impressionable young girl.

Clearly Jason Bullimore had a rapport with his formidable elder sister. She agreed to leave them alone as soon as he suggested it. They heard movements in the rooms upstairs a few seconds later, as if she were confirming that a female like her would never stoop to eavesdropping on the activities of mere policemen.

Her brother threw himself carelessly into an armchair opposite them. Lambert could see him suddenly in his room at an ancient Oxford college, laughing and carefree among the privileged golden youth of his time there. There were, he knew, some men who never moved on from their heady days of breathless development at Oxbridge to the realities of the world outside. "Bad business, this," said Jason Bullimore. "How can I help you?"

Lambert found himself suddenly resentful of this young man's easy social command. "You can be completely frank about your own relationship with Alison Watts. And you can tell us whatever you know of her dealings with other people. Staff and fellow-pupils."

"Students, we tend to call them, once they reach the sixth form. Makes them feel a little more grown up. Well, they are adults, aren't they, once they reach eighteen? But you must be well aware of that. Allows you to question them on their own, doesn't it? Give them the third degree."

The words were delivered a little too rapidly, and the little involuntary laugh at the end confirmed that he was nervous. Lambert decided to chance his arm. "And Alison Watts was a little older than most of the other girls in her group. As you were no doubt aware."

"Was she? I'm not sure I—"

"How long had you known her when she died, Mr Bullimore?"

"Two years. Well, I suppose I'd seen her a little in my first year at Oldford Comp. But I only taught her regularly when she was coming up for GCSEs. I got to know her quite well in her last year, when I was teaching her for A level English in the first year sixth form."

"I see. And at what point did your relationship become more than that of tutor and pupil, Mr Bullimore?"

Suddenly there was electricity coursing through the atmosphere in the room. Hook could feel the hairs on the back of his neck stirring and prickling. But he did not move his hand to them; it was as if any movement in the tableau of three men might break the spell. Bullimore said, "I – I've no idea why you should make such an accusation. If you've been talking to the children at the school, you should certainly know better than to pay heed to their febrile imaginings."

The students had become children again, once it seemed it might be necessary for him to refute their opinions. But he hadn't denied the allegation. Lambert said, "You taught in a public school before you came to Oldford, Mr Bullimore. Why did you choose to leave?"

"Money. Promotion. Comprehensives have more pupils and larger departments. I became Head of English here." The words had come quickly. He had been used to responding to this and other questions about his move to Oldford. No doubt his arguments had usually been accepted.

"No. You didn't become Head of the English Department until you had been at Oldford for a year. When you arrived in the school, you were on no more money than you had been in your previous post. Perhaps slightly less."

Bullimore raised a hand, knocked away the stray curl from his right temple, as if he needed some form of physical release from the tension. "Is this the way the police go about things? Is something which was never proved to be thrown at me for the rest of my life?"

"There was a sexual scandal, wasn't there? You had a relationship with a girl."

"All right, yes. You dig deep, don't you? It was a boys' public school, but they had girls in the sixth form. There was a lot of sexual excitement suddenly flying around."

And a young man not too long out of Oxford who couldn't resist making his contribution to that, thought Lambert. He remembered suddenly Margaret Peplow's jovial remark that you could almost hear the adolescent hormones bouncing about in the sixth form common room at Oldford Comprehensive. He was certain now that the young man writhing before them had been unable to resist that sexual cocktail, despite what should have been a salutary experience in his previous post. "So you had to leave," he said. "No doubt you were told that if you resigned quietly and took yourself somewhere else, there would be no further repercussions. Public schools don't like scandals."

Bullimore nodded miserably. "And Tom Murray didn't ask too many questions when he took me on at Oldford. He was glad enough to have an Oxford English graduate at the time. And I can teach, you know! I know my stuff, and I can get kids interested in literature."

It was probably true, thought Lambert. It was always the best teachers who had the greatest hold over their pupils. And who therefore needed to behave most responsibly. He said, "Were there others here, as well as Alison Watts?"

For a moment, Bullimore seemed to be summoning his resources to deny the suggestion, to challenge them to prove any association with the dead girl. Then his shoulders slumped and he said hopelessly, "Who told you about it? Does everyone know?"

"We can't reveal our sources," said Lambert pompously. It wouldn't do to tell the man that outrageous speculation on

90

his own part had been the main element in extracting this particular piece of information. Far better to spread a belief in police omniscience. "I don't think many people in the school know about your amours. How many have suspected them may be another matter entirely."

"I thought we'd been discreet," said Bullimore hopelessly. He had been transformed in a few moments from a confident, urbane young man into an abject figure. Did it mean that there was more to come; that he had in fact killed the girl to still her tongue? Or was he simply confronting the possibility of a promising career in ruins because of over-active loins?

"When did this affair start?"

"When Alison began in the sixth form. Well, that's when we went to bed together. I'd seen her a couple of times during the summer holidays, but only for a drink. Up beyond Hereford, where we could pretend we'd met by accident if anyone saw us."

But people always thought that no one would, thought Lambert. The naive optimism of human nature in pursuit of sex always surprised him. It upset the judgement of normally careful, even calculating men and women. "And where was this liaison conducted?"

"Here, mostly." Perhaps the surprise they had trained themselves never to show broke through on their faces with the thought of that formidable female upstairs. Jason felt compelled to explain. "I have the place to myself at certain times, you see. Barbara works late three nights of the week. Mondays, Tuesdays and Thursdays. The library is open until eight and she does an hour of cataloguing and ordering after that."

"And your affair was still going on at the time of Alison's death?"

"No." His horror and surprise showed on his face, and they realised that he must have believed that they already knew most of the details of the affair. "It only went on for one term, really." Curious how academics always thought of terms rather than months, thought Lambert. But terms were the landmarks of progress and achievement by which they steered their lives, he supposed.

"Who ended it?"

For a moment the small, handsome features wrestled with a spurt of male pride. Then he said, "She did. When I look back on it now, I think it was just the glamour of being pursued by a tutor which was the main thing for Alison."

"Pity you didn't recognise that when the affair began. It would have saved you a lot of embarrassment and us a lot of work."

"Will – will this have to come out? Surely—"

"Probably. Certainly, if it's connected even remotely with Alison Watts's death."

"It could ruin me."

"You should have thought of that when you put your hand up a schoolgirl's skirt, Mr Bullimore. Especially with your previous record in such matters. The professional implications aren't my concern; you're not the first randy teacher to stray into forbidden areas. But this is a murder investigation. I can't guarantee things like this will be hushed up. Did you strangle Alison Watts?"

The abruptness of the question hit him like a blow in the face, as Lambert had intended it should. "No. No, of course I didn't. How can you—"

"The older man rejected by a pretty young girl. Jealousy setting in. The green-eyed monster, gnawing at the heart, as he sees her with other men. Violence leaping from his mind to his hands as she laughs at her former lover. Classic scenario." This was Bert Hook, coming in on cue, surprising the man with an attack from the quarter where he had least expected it, painting a melodramatic picture which his chief had to admire, even throwing in a phrase from *Othello* for the benefit of the teacher of English.

It was surprisingly effective with Jason Bullimore, who was thrown off balance from the start because his vanity had never permitted him to think of himself as the older man. He faltered, "It – it wasn't like that. Not like that at all."

"Then tell us how it was, Mr Bullimore. In detail. Take all the time you need; we shall stay here as long as is necessary."

The last assurance emerged as a threat, and Lambert was content that Bullimore should take it so. Jason tried to take his time, to re-group. He was supposed to be an expert on words, he reminded himself. He should be able to put a case that these surprisingly knowledgeable men would accept. But his brain would not work

92

as it should with those four watchful eyes unashamedly on his face. He looked at the surface of the coffee table between them, working furiously for concentration: he must not make a mistake now. "Alison was young. She was still growing up. In fact, I saw her develop even during the term or so we had together. I realised eventually that I had been something of a trophy for her." He blushed, keeping his eyes resolutely down. "She said the girls all found me 'dishy'. I think it gave her confidence and an enormous lift when she found that I was attracted to her."

"But it didn't last."

"No. I see now that I shouldn't have expected it to. I had romantic thoughts that we'd continue together, that later, when she'd finished at school, we would be quite open about our partnership. I even toyed with the idea that we might eventually marry."

And they thought women in love were blind, thought Lambert. In his experience, infatuated men were the most gullible and vulnerable of all Cupid's victims. "Did Alison reciprocate these feelings?" he asked quietly.

"No. I don't think so, not now. I kidded myself at the time that she did, but she wouldn't even talk about anything long-term. I was reduced to writing her notes to tell her about my feelings." He smiled wryly. "I even sent her the odd love poem. Not very good, I'm afraid."

Lambert, remembering his own futile efforts at verse for girls in his youth, was filled with a sudden sympathy for this foolish man. "Tell us the rest of the story please."

"There isn't really very much to tell. The sex was good, very good. I kidded myself at the time that there was more to it than some intense sexual couplings. Alison developed through the affair and went on to other things. I see now with the benefit of hindsight that that was probably inevitable."

Lambert wondered if the young man who stared so fixedly at the surface of the low table between them was really as philosophical about this as he now pretended. Passion seldom ebbed at the same rate on both sides; that was why love made life so untidy. Had this man really been able to let go of the affair as completely as he now pretended? He said, "You say

93

that Alison developed and went on to other things. What other things, Mr Bullimore?"

Jason glanced up at them, for the first time in minutes, wondering again how much they knew. They noted the wariness that crept into his face as he said, "I don't know. Really I don't. I got the impression that there were other men around, rather than any specific one. She talked airily about 'playing the field' and 'not being tied down' when I tried to get close to her again. At the time, I thought she was just taunting me: I never saw or heard of any specific new man in her life."

"When did you last see Alison Watts?"

"On Thursday, the twenty-second of July, in school. There was school on the morning of Friday the twenty-third, of course, the last day of term, but as it happened I wasn't teaching Alison's group that day."

The answer had come promptly, perhaps a little too quickly. But then he must have expected to be asked this, must have thought about how he would answer. Lambert's grey eyes bored into his face, testing his honesty, trying hard to see what he was holding back. Jason found this moment of silent, unashamed assessment the worst of all. Eventually Lambert said, "Alison had a boyfriend of her own age."

He nodded. "Young Jamie Allen. Bright lad – should make Oxbridge, if he wants to. She was with him before we had our affair. I suppose I should have felt guilty, but we seemed somehow to be set apart from that. I never took Jamie as a serious rival; I thought of it as the kind of adolescent boy-girl relationship which had been transcended by our more intense affair. She went on seeing him all through the term when we were meeting here – it just seemed something quite separate."

"And a useful cover for your clandestine relationship, no doubt," said Lambert drily. Yet he didn't really think there was much calculation in this man; despite his intelligence, he was in some senses more vulnerable than Jamie Allen. And thus possibly more dangerous; all cornered animals, even the most civilised, can turn violent. "Jamie claims that Alison was still seeing him at the time of her disappearance. Is that correct?"

For a moment, Bullimore's too-revealing face showed the hurt of the idea that this gangling youth could have retained some sort of relationship with the girl long after his own tempestuous intrigue had been concluded. "Yes. As far as I know, that is. Alison always said that she needed Jamie to come back to, whatever was happening in the rest of her life. She never cut him off. Whether she was just making use of him, you'll need to decide for yourself." It was the first shaft of real bitterness he had permitted himself in speaking of the dead girl, and he glanced quickly at their faces, as if aware of a mistake.

"Do you think Jamie killed Alison?"

"No. Of course not."

"Someone killed her. You say you didn't. If not Jamie, who else?"

He shook his head doggedly. "I don't know. Perhaps someone she only met on the day she died."

It was the solution all those who had been close to Alison Watts seemed to want. Lambert, looking at the severely discomforted Jason Bullimore, was more than ever convinced that it wasn't the real answer. Something, some tiny detail, had jarred in his mind, but he couldn't pinpoint the moment.

Chapter Eleven

DI RUSHTON was as spruce and businesslike as usual when they reached the murder room. He might live on his own now, his marriage a victim of the demands of the job, but his striped shirt was as immaculately laundered as any man's in the station. Christopher Rushton had always been a modern man, a man who had shared the domestic tasks with his mate, a determined feminist in a force that had had to learn the facts of equality slowly and laboriously. In short, a great loss to the world of marriage; most of the women about the station were agreed on that, though none had rushed in to claim this prize when it became available.

He came forward a little self-importantly with the information they had requested. His every movement proclaimed that even if it was Saturday and less dedicated policemen were at home with their families, Detective Inspector Rushton, like crime, paid no attention to the days of the week. "No problem tracing that phone number. It's a singles club. Cotswold Rendezvous, they call themselves. 'The professional introduction agency for professional people', their advertising copy says."

"Now what would a pretty young girl be doing with a number like that in her school locker?" said Lambert. "Girls of that age don't use agencies."

"We don't know that she did," Hook pointed out. "Anyone could have put that slip of paper in there."

"Indeed. But it's difficult to see how it could have got into a locked metal cubicle like that by accident. Anyone who put it there did it for a reason. And what reason could anyone have for doing that? There was no guarantee that it would be found. It was stuck right at the back and out of sight. If I'd been planting it, I'd have wanted to make sure it was a bit more obvious."

Rushton cleared his throat, picked self-consciously at the already immaculate cuffs of his shirt. "Some of these introduction agencies are not quite what they seem, John." The first name came out a little too deliberately; it was only because Lambert had insisted upon it that he used it at all. Chris Rushton was a man more comfortable with the handles of rank or the simple 'Sir' than with forenames: even the ubiquitous 'Guv'nor' of the force did not come easily to him.

"Knocking shops, are they?" said Lambert. "Well, of course, you'd know more about that than me, Chris. Or even old Bert, I expect." He produced his most innocent and open smile.

"I haven't sampled any of these singles clubs, you understand, John," Rushton said hastily. Because he was basically a humourless man, he found it difficult to deal with these two old sweats in tandem. "But you must be aware that there have been instances of businesses which supply women for immoral purposes under the guise of being introduction agencies."

"Knocking shops," said Lambert with satisfaction. "Run without the expense and danger of setting up premises as brothels and inviting police interest. Of course I'm aware of it. I'm also aware of the frustration of the vice squad that nothing has been proved as yet. Not on our patch."

Rushton nodded, wondering how to push his ideas without giving the impression that he knew more than he cared to admit about singles clubs and the like. "The suspicion is that girls have been recruited to provide sexual services for men with the money to pay. Young girls, not established prostitutes. And young men of eighteen to twenty-one. Children too, perhaps, for the pederasts in our splendid community. But it's all very vague."

Lambert nodded. "It's a potentially lucrative trade, catering for people's sexual preferences, especially if you can provide a comprehensive service. And who are the men you think might be behind this enterprising development?" He had his own names in mind, from his exchanges with other senior officers, but he was curious to know how much had seeped down as far as Inspector level. A good CID officer was usually aware of the serious villainies abroad in the area, whatever his sources of information might be.

DI Ruston did not disappoint him. "The rumour is that Eddie Hurst is developing a ring of sexual services. But he keeps far enough away from things to make it very difficult to get evidence."

"Hurst the worst," said Hook, producing one of the schoolboy rhymes beloved of frustrated policemen.

Lambert's nose wrinkled fastidiously at the banality of it. "Yes. If we've got to have rhyming slang, I've always thought it would have been more appropriate if that bugger had been called Hunt."

Rushton was not quite sure how to react to this. He said hastily, "Of course, Cotswold Rendezvous may have nothing to do with Eddie Hurst. It may be a perfectly straightforward and respectable introduction agency. I only mentioned other possibilities because you invited us to speculate about how Alison Watts came to have this 'phone number, and—"

"Yes. Quite so." Lambert's face brightened suddenly as he glanced round the almost deserted Saturday murder room. "Well, there's only one way I can see to test the water," he said cheerfully.

Bert Hook as usual was on to his chief's train of thought faster than anyone else. "You mean we need to test the agency out," he mused happily.

"Plant someone," said Lambert.

"Someone single?"

"Perhaps divorced or separated. We need the typical customer if they're not to suspect."

"But personable."

"And not too old. Early thirties, would you say?"

"Absolutely. And with the right bearing and appearance. Must be able to pass himself off effortlessly as a professional man."

"Mean inspector rank, I'd say."

"Agreed . . . I wonder who could possibly do the job?"

Two beaming faces turned their full bonhomie upon DI Christopher Rushton. Two pairs of eyebrows raised themselves as if drawn by a single string.

Rushton might have retarded humour cells, but he was not stupid. Indeed, he was an intelligent and occasionally resourceful officer, and he had seen the way this bizarre cross-talk act was going long before its conclusion. "If you should mean me, it's not on!" he said in consternation. "I couldn't possibly carry it off. And besides—"

"Chance I never had," said Bert Hook sadly. "Meeting young women at police expense. Pocket full of money and introduction to a pretty woman. Good thing the taxpayer doesn't know what his money's being spent on."

"And the chances are the whole thing is perfectly innocent. Probably the lucky man selected for the task will meet some luscious but frustrated young woman who'll be just dying to get at his lean young body and have her way with him. Chance of a lifetime."

"For the man lucky enough to be selected," said Hook dolefully. "Only wish I wasn't too old and too ugly and too married to put myself forward for the job."

The two faces beamed again at an inspector who was now full of trepidation. He had always found it difficult to know when his leg was being tweaked. His rise in rank had been a protection against that: in a service acutely conscious of hierarchy, not many people were in a position to extract the urine from an inspector. But he could never be sure of his ground with these two; old John Lambert seemed at times to encourage an unseemly levity. And that Bert Hook had turned down the chance of promotion to inspector rank, years ago, as well as doing an Open University degree now: one could never be certain of a man like that.

There seemed to Chris Rushton an awful possibility that they might be serious in their suggestion. "I couldn't possibly do it," he said desperately. "I look far too much like a policeman. It would be a dead giveaway. And—"

He stopped. The grins before him had broadened, like twin Cheshire cats leering at him out of Alice's trees. All three of them knew he didn't look like a policeman. He had prided himself upon that in the past. With his slim build, his brown hair without a trace of grey, his keen hazel eyes, his smart dark suits and fashionable ties, he was more dynamic sales manager than detective, he looked much more the young executive than the dutiful police bureaucrat he was in fact.

99

Lambert set his head on one side, considered his detective inspector critically for a moment. "Wouldn't spot him as a copper in a million years. Would you, Bert?"

"Never. Industrial whizz-kid maybe. Future company chairman, perhaps. But copper, never."

They turned their heads and beamed for a moment at each other, then turned their gaze in unison back to their victim. Rushton found it most disconcerting. He said, "But seriously, Superintendent Lambert—"

"John."

"John, then. You can't really expect me to undertake this – this masquerade."

"Expect, Chris, yes. But not compel. No one would wish to force you into undertaking such an interesting and responsible mission. This needs a volunteer, of course. I should have to get permission from above to spend good money on such an unusual enterprise. But if I were to be asked to suggest a name for such a perilous and ultimately prestigious exploit, I could think of no one more appropriate or deserving than your good self. Now that the possibility has presented itself, of course."

"Lots of kudos, I should think, for the man who brings it off." Bert Hook kept his gaze resolutely upon the wall behind Rushton as he mused. He shook his head sadly at the thought of the opportunity which was not for him. "Promotion, I shouldn't wonder."

"High profile, certainly. Bound to reach the ears of the Chief Constable, if someone brings it off," said Lambert. "Indeed, I should think it no more than my duty to make sure he was aware of the versatility of an officer who could bring us the information we need from a situation like this."

They were making fun of him. Chris Rushton knew that now, quite clearly. But they might still be serious about him doing this under-cover job. And he pricked up his ears at the mention of versatility. It was not a quality which had been noted in him before. Knowledgeable, yes, especially about police procedures and the intricacies of the law; diligent, certainly; and reliable, that old police standby that had been the most important of all in carrying him to the Inspectorate; but versatile? That had certainly not figured in his previous reports and reviews. If he could add versatility to his cv then who knew where he might go? "Er,. what exactly would be involved?" he said.

Lambert tried not to look like a fisherman reaching for the net to bring ashore this fine fish which had attached itself to his line. He pursed his lips. "You'd just have to be yourself, I suppose, Chris. An attractive young professional man, in search of female companionship. If it's innocent, if you're offered no more than an introduction to a woman who fits your requirements, as outlined on your form, then you leave it at that. Unless, of course, the lady in question proves genuinely attractive to you, in which case your future relationship would be an entirely private matter." The smiles were back, Rushton noticed. "On the other hand, if there proved to be sinister overtones to the Cotswold Rendezvous and you were offered services of a dubious nature, we should need all the information we could get about a criminal enterprise. You would have to use your judgement as an officer to decide how that might be obtained."

"Rumpety at public expense, I shouldn't wonder!" said Hook with relish. "A consummation devoutly to be wished, eh, Chris?"

"You must excuse this excess of vulgarity in a junior officer," said Lambert magisterially. "He's studying literature, you see – it often seems to have that effect."

"I – I wouldn't want to get in too deep, you see," said Rushton.

"No, I can quite see that. It's a situation in which one might need to – well, to know when to withdraw. If that's the right word." Lambert savoured it for a moment with a resolutely straight face.

Rushton felt the blood pounding in his head, felt himself floundering but excited at the possibility of an attractive woman, to his own specifications, supplied at police expense. These two silly old buggers might be laughing at him now, but the laugh would be on them if this was all above board and they found they had paid his expenses to meet a pretty girl. He'd been very lonely since Anne left and the divorce came through, though he couldn't admit it to the coarse men around the station who thought he was a stallion roaming free. And if this wasn't straightforward and there

101

were darker forces at work behind Cotswold Rendezvous? Well, if he played a vital part in unmasking a vice ring, that couldn't do his promotion prospects any harm at all. If the deskbound DI Rushton emerged as dynamic and full of initiative, that would open a few important eyes. Versatile as well as reliable? It was an intoxicating compound: not least to the one who now drank it. "I'll do it!" he heard himself saying.

Self-knowledge, an awareness of his own strengths and weaknesses, is perhaps the most important quality of all for a senior officer. Christopher Rushton had forgotten all about that.

Tom Murray was playing with his two children in the garden of his Cotswold home when the call came. He heard the phone ring in the house, but left it for his wife to answer, as he always did at the weekends. She knew her role in filtering calls to do with the school. The headmaster would make the ten-mile journey to Oldford Comprehensive on Saturday or Sunday only if there was a real emergency, and they were few and far between. It was Ros's role to protect his privacy.

Down in the orchard beyond the formal garden, his face clouded as he heard the distant ringing through the open windows. The call from that sinister man in Cheltenham last night had ensured he had not had much sleep. It had been the merest chance that he had taken the call himself. What the man had said had set alarm bells ringing in his head which he had still not been able to silence. He pushed his laughing daughter gently on the swing, trying to still his uneasiness with the slow rhythm of the movement.

Ros was apologetic but unworried as she came down the garden in the October sunshine. Her husband's weekend was going to be disturbed, but it was nothing to cause him any personal anxiety. "It's the police," she said. "A Detective Sergeant Hook. He and his boss would like a few words with you about that poor dead girl. 'In the light of their continuing enquiries', he said. Shall I ask them to come out here?"

"No. I'll go into the school. Or the police station at Oldford, if they like." Anywhere but here, in his wife's innocent presence.

102

He did not want this house tainted with what he had done, if it had to come out.

His daughter had slipped off the swing and gone back up the garden, chatting happily to her mother. The seat swung emptily, pointlessly in front of him as he stared at it.

DI Rushton sat in front of his computer in the deserted murder room, wondering quite what he had let himself in for. Lambert had disappeared as soon as he agreed to make himself a candidate for Cotswold Rendezvous, to clear the move with the vice squad and the Chief Constable. Chris had an unpleasant feeling that the chief was making sure the die was cast before he could change his mind.

He was wondering quite what he had let himself in for when he found himself contending with an unexpected visitor. The civilian who was manning the Saturday morning desk at the front of the station brought in a woman in a shabby coat which was a little too long for her. Her eyes were red and swollen, despite the make-up she had applied to try to disguise them. There was a yellow-green bruise on her temple, from an impact which had taken place some time ago; perhaps four days, Rushton's experienced, automatic eye told him. "This is Mrs Watts," said the grey-haired man who had ushered her in. He spoke apologetically, feeling perhaps he should have headed her off, should not have let her penetrate to this inner sanctum of detection. He was right: there could have been personal effects or photographs here which would have brought distress to the parent of a murder victim.

Fortunately, there was nothing, in this case. Even the dead girl's clothes had been safely bagged away in cupboards, and there had been no point in pinning up enlargements of a ten-week old corpse. Rushton hastily took Kate Watts into the small office just off the main area of the murder room and asked what he could do for her.

"It's about Alison," she said abruptly as soon as she was seated. She was going to get this out quickly, before her pounding heart drove her to reconsider her decision to come here. "There are things you don't know yet. Things I feel you ought to know. They may have nothing to do with her death, mind—" She dissolved

103

suddenly into fresh tears, abject, apologetic, incoherent, just when she most wanted to get the words out and be done with this.

Chris Rushton said clumsily, "Take your time, m' dear. There's no hurry." He came round the desk and put his hand on the shoulder of the rough, worn coat. He wished desperately that there was a woman officer around, who could take this pathetic figure into her arms and hold her, if it came to it. But he was eager, too; there is enough of the hunter in all detectives to make them excited at the thought of new revelations in a case which had seemed to be going nowhere. He waited until the sobbing abated, until the shoulders beneath the worn tweed moved less actively, then said gently, in the Gloucestershire accent he thought he had lost, "What is it you wanted to tell us, m'dear?"

"It's Robert," she said. He had to think for a moment to remember whom she might mean. Her husband, of course, the man who had struck that blow that was now healing, and others too, no doubt. Even as he made the connection, she was going on, her breath coming in great uneven gasps that she could not control. "He – he kissed her. Did other things. He – what's the word, you have a word for it—"

"Abused her?"

"Yes. That's it. Abused her. That's what he did. Robert. Her own father – well stepfather." She sounded as if she had to go on repeating the facts, to convince herself these awful things had happened.

"When was this, Mrs Watts?"

She looked at him, wide eyes wet with alarm. She had not thought that the time would be important. For her, it was as vivid as yesterday. The appalling nature of the actions seemed to make all other considerations trivial. "I don't know. Well, yes, I do, I suppose, if you need it." She thought furiously for a moment, casting a hand impatiently through her wild hair, as if it was a curtain in front of the picture. "Two years ago. More. Two and a half. Alison would have been sixteen at the time."

"Did this happen on more than one occasion? Did the abuse go on for any length of time, Mrs Watts?"

She was curiously consoled by this word 'abuse'. She had expected grosser, more explicit words, had herself thought in

104

terms of them. It didn't sound so bad, somehow, when you could blanket all those nightmare images under a word like that. "It went on for a while, I think. But I don't know, really. Alison never told me. I only found out about it last night."

He took her as gently as he could through a few of the details, stopping short of the squalor of whether there had been full penetration. He did not even ask her whether there had been any degree of consent on the girl's part. That was something to be investigated with the offender, in due course.

He made her have a mug of hot tea before she left, though she would not accept the heaped spoons of sugar which were the standard police palliative. "Putting on too much weight, I am!" she sniffed, with a pathetic attempt at a smile at this strange, awkward young man who had been so kind and understanding.

DI Rushton commiserated with Kate Watts as everyone else had done about her daughter, as they waited for a brief statement to be typed for her signature. He told her they were going to find out who had killed Alison, and she believed him. He arranged that a car would take her back to the hostel whence she had come, and she was grateful.

Finally, he made her promise to keep away from Robert Watts, the husband she had just put so firmly in the frame for the murder of her daughter.

Chapter Twelve

ROBERT Watts was not at home. There was no sign of the dead girl's father at One, The Lawns. The shabby little box of a house rang empty as they hammered at the door, and none of the curious neighbours who watched the two large men had any idea as to the whereabouts of the occupant. They left a message that he should contact Oldford CID as soon as he returned and walked back through the unkempt front garden, which was so much of a contrast with the obsessive neatness of the Bullimore garden they had visited earlier in the day.

Lambert drove the old Vauxhall the threequarters of a mile to Oldford Comprehensive School, along the suburban streets which must have been Alison Watts's route to the school over the years in which she had grown from gawky schoolgirl with a brace on her teeth to fatally attractive young woman. These were roads lined with quiet, respectable houses, where children played on the lawns and the gables were clothed with the green of ivy and the fire of Virginia creeper in its autumn glory.

Tom Murray was waiting for them at the deserted school. They saw his face peering anxiously from the headmaster's office as they drew up, and he was outside the big double doors by the time Lambert and Hook reached the main entrance to the school. He had on a new pair of blue denim trousers and a green sweater, an outfit proclaiming that this was a Saturday, that he should have been enjoying a well-earned rest, that he had come in to the school only because of his strong sense of duty. He tried to emphasise the point lightly with his first words. "I was happy to come in to offer whatever help I can," he said. "Though I can't think I have anything useful to contribute myself. But perhaps you want an overview of her school life and her companions here, and I shall be happy of course to provide it."

He was talking too much, probing nervously to find out why they had wanted to see him. Lambert let him talk, punctuating his flow with nothing more than the occasional grunt, affirmatory or non-committal by turns. Murray took them up the stairs and into his room, shutting the door behind them as carefully as if there had been the normal crowded school of weekdays behind it. Habit, perhaps, thought Hook. Or apprehension.

Still they did not help him. Murray gestured to the two armchairs, then perched on the edge of his desk and said nervously, "Of course, I'd like to offer you coffee, but I'm afraid that on a Saturday—"

"Mr Murray, why did you supervise the clearing of Alison Watts's locker yourself?" Lambert had struck at last, abruptly, without any sort of polite preamble.

"I – I don't recall . . . Her steel locker, in the basement, you mean? But that was months ago, at the end of July, I suppose."

"Yes. When Alison was first declared a missing person. The locker was opened, presumably to see if it offered any clue as to where the girl might have gone, but without any police presence. You took away the contents of her locker yourself."

"But there were only books. And a few exercise books and a magazine, if I can recall things accurately at this length of time. Nothing that gave us any clue as to why Alison might have disappeared so suddenly, unfortunately. I can't think why you—"

"But you cleared the locker yourself, without the attendance of any experienced police officer, who might have given a more expert view on what might or might not have been important in the case of a missing person."

"But this is ridiculous. All I was trying to do was to move quickly, to ascertain as fast as possible whether there was anything in my school which might help to allay fears about a missing sixth form student. To suggest otherwise is outrageous. Indeed—"

"No one has suggested anything, Mr Murray. We are asking questions, that is all. Any unusual behaviour pattern in relation to a murder victim is of interest to us. More than that: it is our duty to investigate it."

Tom Murray lifted his hands from the edges of the desk beside him and folded them deliberately across his chest. Two tell-tale mists of moisture remained for a moment on the polished wood of the desk behind him, then disappeared into the air of the quiet room. He tried to be deliberate, as if dealing as he had so many times with an obtuse parent. He even attempted to force a trace of sarcasm into his voice. "So you think it's unusual for a head teacher to show concern for a missing pupil? To be anxious to find out as soon as possible whether there is anything around which might allay the fears of parents frantic with worry? To get a school thrown into chaos moving forward again on the education of the rest of its pupils, which is our prime reason for existence?"

Where before Lambert had interrupted him, had refused to let him develop a thought, he now let Murray wander on with his increasingly desperate catalogue, until his rhetoric failed for want of a reaction to spur it on. Then the Superintendent said, "But it was the beginning of the summer holidays, wasn't it, when the girl was registered as missing? No disruption of the school timetable then, surely?" Then, while Murray mentally pawed the air, he came back to his original, unanswered question. "Would you say it was normal for a busy headmaster to take away the contents of the locker, Mr Murray? Even if you didn't think to wait for a police presence, wouldn't it have been more natural, more sensible even, to leave the investigation of the locker's contents to someone in daily contact with Alison Watts? To Mrs Peplow, for instance, who has charge of sixth form studies, or to one of the girl's other teachers? Even to some of her fellow students, who might best appreciate the origin and significance of anything personal within the contents?"

For a moment, Tom almost said that the teachers and students had all gone off on holiday in July, that he had investigated things himself because he had been the only one around. But it had not been so. The news of the girl's disappearance had brought both staff and students into the school in that first week of the holiday. These men would check, as they seemed to check everything, and find that he was lying. And then they would want to know why. He said sullenly, feeling the inadequacy of the words dry in his

108

mouth, "It might have been unusual, I suppose. I can't say why I emptied the locker myself, at this distance of time. All I know is that I was anxious to clear things up, to see if there was any clue I could find as to where the girl had gone."

"I see. And did you discover anything of interest?"

"No. I told you that. There was nothing except textbooks and exercise books. And a women's magazine. If there had been anything, I'd have brought it to the notice of the police at the time."

"Yes. Of course you would. Well, it will be of interest to you to know that you didn't clear the locker of its contents completely, Mr Murray. It might have been better to have invoked police assistance at the time, after all."

They were no more than six feet from him, and they saw fear flash into his too-revealing blue eyes, then the suspicion that this might be some kind of trick. "What do you mean? The caretaker and I cleared the damned locker completely at the time. He'll tell you that there was nothing left in there when—"

"Mr Phillips was present when we investigated the locker this morning. Indeed, he opened it up for us. It was apparently empty, as you say. But we did find this one scrap of paper, trapped in the corner behind the single shelf at the top of the locker."

Lambert produced the tiny scrap of grubby paper like a triumphant magician from his jacket pocket. Hook resisted the temptation to applaud. "This may of course have been placed in the locker by person or persons unknown since you emptied it. But as there was no sign of any forced entry, that would have necessitated a key. I think the probability is that you simply missed this."

Murray's eyes were fixed still on the hand that held the scrap of paper. But he could not see what was written upon it. He said harshly, "Well, what of it? You're going to tell me you hold the key to the murder of Alison Watts in your hand, are you? The Great Detective reveals his triumph!" He tried a sardonic laugh, but it emerged as a breathy, uneven chuckle. Watching the headmaster's discomfort, Hook reflected that the chief could be quite a ham, when it suited him. But he was making this bugger dance to his tune.

Lambert said drily, "If I'd had the evidence, we'd have made an arrest, Mr Murray. But it's only a matter of time. This is merely a telephone number."

Again, there was apprehension as well as enquiry in Murray's face. This time he could not even attempt irony as he said, "A significant telephone number?"

"We don't know, yet. But I think it may prove to be so, and so does Sergeant Hook." He paused. He had been about to tell Murray about Cotswold Rendezvous, to see if it brought any reaction from the man while he had him squirming. But he couldn't reveal the information, if they were going to send in Rushton to test out whether the singles agency was merely a front for something darker. Instead, he said, "We have been told that Miss Watts went off into Gloucester or Cheltenham on Friday evenings, and sometimes at the weekend as well. Do you have any idea where she might have gone on these occasions?"

"No. Why should I? Are you sure that she went to those towns? And why shouldn't she anyway? Why should there be anything dubious about her visits?" His speech was jerky, unnatural, reflecting the desperate improvisation of his thoughts.

"You didn't see her yourself in either of those towns?"

"No. Never. Is there any reason why I should have?"

"No reason at all that we know of, Mr Murray. But it's sensible for us to ask." But he hadn't denied that he might have been in the same area, they noticed, as a wholly innocent man might have done. "We shall go on asking people about those visits of Alison's, until we find someone who knows what she was about, you see."

"Yes. I see that. Well, I can't help you, I'm afraid."

"We'll leave you, then. Thank you for your help."

They saw his white face watching them from the window as they drove away, as it had earlier watched their arrival. Neither of them thought that Thomas Murray, MA, FRSA, Headmaster of Oldford Comprehensive, would get much sleep on that Saturday night.

"I – I've drafted this out," said Rushton diffidently. He handed John Lambert a half-sheet of paper covered with neat handwriting, watching hard for any sort of amusement on the Superintendent's face. It was a requirement, apparently, that you wrote up yourself and your requirements for this damned agency; Cotswold Rendezvous took the standard details of age, height and so on, but they wanted to know 'how you see yourself and your aspirations'. Load of bloody nonsense: he wished he'd never got involved, but it was too late now. The idea of planting him had been approved by the police hierarchy with uncharacteristic speed.

Lambert hadn't seen Chris Rushton's handwriting for a long time. Normally all his communications were via his computer; perhaps he did not want to leave any possibility of this effort being preserved or reproduced for other eyes. While Rushton cringed, Lambert read aloud, " 'Frank Lloyd. Professional man, early thirties, polite and active, no ties. Seeks female company, initially for outings to cinema and theatre.' " He looked across at Hook and shook his head sadly. "Not a trend-setter, is he, our Frank?"

Hook shook his serious, experienced head, pursing his lips in thought to avoid any suggestion of a smile. "Not quite the kind of entry I'd thought of. We want quick results, don't we? So I think we need to sell our very promising candidate a little harder." He produced his own effort, staring hard at the paper, knowing that if he caught the eye of either Rushton or Lambert he would dissolve into helpless and indecorous laughter. He took a deep breath and read, " 'Raunchy male, early thirties but with the stamina of a younger man, seeks leggy, curvaceous younger woman with no inhibitions and lots of invention.' " He looked up at the wall above Rushton's appalled head and kept his gaze steadily upon it. "Short and to the point, I thought. As you said, sir, we need to get things moving if our man is to test whether there are knocking shop possibilities in this."

"Yes, I see what you're getting at." Lambert turned to Rushton. "I think Bert is right – you need to sell your undoubted attractions a little harder, Chris." He turned back to Hook. "Do we need to stress that he's heterosexual, do you think? We don't want to land him in any embarrassing situations."

Hook shook his head. "I've studied the adverts in the paper carefully and I don't think it's necessary, so long as you mention girls and imply that you're a stud." He looked for the first time at

111

Rushton. "Of course, if there is real corruption and these people are supplying sex for money, it might bring it into the open more quickly if you were prepared to say that you were interested in young men or boys. But we couldn't really ask you to—"

Rushton suddenly found the tongue which had been paralysed with disbelief. And it shouted, "You're not saying that! Or anything like it! Or any of these other things!"

Lambert intervened, his face resolutely serious and anxious. "All right, Chris. We all know you're a sensitive, caring chap. But it may not pay to stress that. We need to get things moving, as Bert says. You're probably too reticent about your virtues. I've looked at these adverts in the *Meeting Point* columns of our local press, and the men seem to have no modesty. They proclaim themselves as 'hunks', looking for curvaceous women who 'want to be shown a thing or two'; then they say in the next phrase that they have a good sense of humour – seems contradictory to me."

Hook was enjoying himself, he hoped not too visibly. "But we do need to state what Chris has to offer, and what he is looking for in a partner. Or partners."

Rushton said desperately, "What he *purports* to be looking for. Don't forget that this is all play-acting. In the line of duty."

"Oh, strictly in the line of duty," said Bert. "But . . . rumpety on the house! Nice work, if you can get it. And I expect you probably will."

In the end they compromised. 'Frank Lloyd' was to be a handsome professional man in his early thirties. Divorced and without any ties. And looking for attractive female company 'with no holds barred'. It took them some time to get Rushton to agree the last phrase; he eventually sanctioned it, reluctantly, on the grounds that it was much less offensive than the other phrases he was offered in the same vein.

They left Chris Rushton looking thoroughly uneasy and managed not to laugh outright until they were safely out of the station.

On that early autumn Saturday, the night fell in early and chill after a perfect day. At six-thirty Barbara Bullimore switched the central heating on in the quiet house for the first time since

112

spring and agreed with her brother that winter could not now be far away.

Physically as well as mentally, they were an ill-assorted pair, this brother and sister, whose parents had been prosperous working class in the palmy 'sixties days of full employment. Barbara had been a bright, lumpy girl at the all-girls grammar school. They had not meant to hold her back, had meant to do their very best for both of their children. But a place at the Institute of Librarians College had seemed a splendid achievement, for a girl. And when they were told that her bright, handsome younger brother might even make Oxford or Cambridge, that had seemed so dazzling a prospect that he had naturally received all the attention and all the encouragement, from his loving older sister as well as his astonished parents.

And Jason had made it to Oxford. It had been more expensive than any of them had anticipated, even with the student grant which was supposed to cover most things but didn't. And the golden boy had done well in that strange, hot-house environment, justifying all the sacrifices of his doting family. Barbara had done well, too, passing out third in her year at the College of Librarianship. But that was when Jason was completing his first year at Oxford, and her success, though registered, had been celebrated only in a modest way within the family.

Barbara did not mind. She was a self-effacing girl, devoted to the family and taking as much vicarious delight in her more extrovert brother's successes as anyone. When her beloved parents had died within a year of each other, it had seemed natural that she would set up house with Jason, who welcomed the arrangement in his elegant, easy-going way. Now that his parents were gone, he missed the unquestioning affection and admiration they had bestowed upon him; Barbara, though she often mimed the disapproval of a watchful older sister, supplied that gap in his life.

Barbara enjoyed her job and she was good at it. She was not gay, but she was happier working with women than with men. Her formidable physical appearance meant that she had few male sexual advances to contend with, and she had long since decided that she liked life that way. Jason might behave stupidly sometimes, but he was bright and interesting. She smiled proudly over his progress and indulgently over his faults. He might be a young fool at times, but he was her young fool.

And tonight he had cooked the meal for them. It was only a casserole, and in truth he had followed her recipe. But he had bought the ingredients himself that morning, and she had kept out of the kitchen while he had busied himself like an enthusiastic child over the preparation of the various items and their consignment for the rest of the day to the slow cooker. She had busied herself with the thorough digging and weeding of the new rose bed they had planned for the back garden. When she came down from her shower, he was setting the casserole dish proudly on its mat in the middle of the table.

They had eaten for several minutes with no more than the briefest of small talk when Jason said, "They were thorough this morning, that superintendent and his sergeant. The fuzz aren't all Mister Plods, after all."

It was the first time he had been prepared to talk about the exchange. He had been non-committal when they left, and she had not pressed him. She had been dying to know what they had said, how far they had pressed him, how much they already knew, but the weight of her role in this partnership had been too strong for her to push him. Now she said, "Pried into everything, I expect. Well, it's their job after all. When there's been a murder, you'd expect it."

"Yes. They seem absolutely sure it's a murder. I suppose the forensic people will have confirmed that for them. I don't know much about the details."

Not for the first time, she wondered just how much Jason did know about the death of this wretched girl. And how much of that he had revealed to the police. "Did you find out whether they think it was someone who picked her up on that night – someone who hadn't seen her before?" She had seen his face wince at the idea of Alison Watts being a casual pick-up for some man. He still cared something for the girl, this vulnerable, intelligent, but stupid brother of hers. "I tried to find out the way they were thinking before you came back from the shops, but I didn't get very far."

"No. They're much better at gathering information than at dishing it out, those two. They – they knew all about me, Sis."

He only addressed her like that when he was prepared for

114

conversational intimacies. Normally she warmed to the term; tonight it sent a chill into her blood. "You mean they knew about the trouble you had in Wiltshire?" They had never mentioned the school by name since he had left, as if such detail might make the memory even more painful and embarrassing.

"Yes." He turned a piece of shin-beef over on his plate, then impaled it violently upon his fork.

"It wasn't from me. I didn't tell them."

"No. No, I know you wouldn't have told them, Sis. But they knew, from somewhere. They'd gone back into my records, I think. Or someone had told them about it – I don't know who. I suppose the headmaster knows about it, but I didn't think anyone else did."

You poor, benighted boy, she thought. How can you be so clever, and yet so ignorant of the way people behave? Scandal travels far faster than any other disease among bored people. Barbara knew that. She heard the women she worked with, women she liked in other respects, passing around titbits of gossip whenever they were to hand. She would have wagered that most of the staff at Oldford Comprehensive knew the circumstances of Jason's arrival there, by now. She said quietly, "Did they press you about it?"

"Not much, no. They were more interested in my relationship with Alison Watts."

It was his way of telling her that they knew about his affair with the dead girl, about that awful mess which she had found out about at the time, when he had thought he would be able to keep it secret from her.

Barbara tried to sound deliberately low-key; in the months after her disappearance, Alison Watts had never been mentioned in this house; it had suited her that way. "And how much did they know about you and that girl?"

"Everything. Well, I think everything." For the first time, Jason wondered if the officers had not really known as much about the affair as he had supposed, whether he had really needed to reveal the sexual details of his short-lived passion for Alison Watts. "They asked me all about it, and I thought it best to tell them."

"But Jason . . . that must make you a suspect, in their book."

115

"Yes. They more or less said that. But there didn't seem to be any way round it, Sis. They aren't fools, those two. I thought it best to let them have the truth."

She could see him twenty years ago as a nine-year-old in short trousers, confessing the facts of some small sin, expecting inwardly to be praised for telling the truth like a good, honest boy. He always had been praised, too, in those days. Perhaps that was what had made it so hard for him to come to terms with the dangers of real life, in an adult world. When you confessed things there, forgiveness wasn't automatic, and there was a price to pay. She said only, "I expect you're right. They'd have found out for themselves, from someone, even if you hadn't told them."

She felt a little pang of irrational jealousy that these strangers, the police, might know more than she did about what her beloved brother had done with that young minx. But she had never wanted to know the full, squalid details of what Jason had done with that pretty, vapid creature. Men had needs, and Jason had his instincts like the rest of them. But she didn't want to picture what happened when he indulged himself like that.

Jason said, "I told them it had ended long before she disappeared, and I think they believed me." There was no use telling her that it hadn't been just a sordid little tumble, that he had hoped that he and Alison might one day get married. She wouldn't understand, and it would only annoy her. Barbara's contempt was not to be undertaken lightly.

She said, "Do the police have any idea yet of exactly when she died, or who killed her, do you think?"

He shook his head. "I don't think so. But they don't say much. I think they believe she died shortly after she disappeared, but they don't have a time and a place. At least, if they do, they weren't telling me. I suppose it could still be someone we don't even know."

It could. But Barbara didn't think the CID men thought that. Jason was too sanguine, as usual. She wondered just how deeply the police suspected her bright and vulnerable brother.

Chapter Thirteen

THE inquest on Alison Watts was conducted on Monday morning. It was routine stuff, save for the evidence of identification being by means of dental records. The Coroner expressed his sympathy with the bereaved parents, though only Kate Watts was in court to hear the verdict of Murder by Person or Persons Unknown. Lambert, by prior arrangement with the Coroner's Officer, gave only the briefest account of the present progress of the police investigation into the crime. No need to put a chief suspect on his guard. Or in this case, no need to reassure an unknown killer that there was as yet no chief suspect.

Lambert lunched at home, because Christine's part-time teaching post now left her free on Mondays. He was so preoccupied with the case that he did not notice that his wife was unusually quiet over their soup and sandwiches. He talked a little about the investigation to her, as once he would not have done. Perhaps that was because she had known the girl when she was much younger, or because of the school environment which surrounded this victim. His teacher wife answered him mainly in monosyllables.

He had forgotten that his wife had been to the hospital that morning. He did not even ask her about what the specialist had said. Christine had been all ready to tell him that the mastectomy she had undergone six months previously had been a complete success; that there was no sign of the cancer recurring; that she now did not have to attend the hospital for a whole year. But John Lambert had forgotten that it was today that was her big day. It was like the old times, when he was young, when she had not seen him for days when a case was developing, when he had scarcely seen his babies growing into toddlers, and their marriage had almost foundered on the CID rocks.

Nothing like that would happen now, she consoled herself bleakly. She tried to smile at herself, to find it reassuring that the old John Lambert that she had married and loved was still not too far beneath the surface. And at four o'clock, he rang, as she had known he would eventually. He was full of apologies, full of relief that her news was so good. She told him it did not matter that he had forgotten it at lunch-time, and settled down with the crossword and the television to wait for him to arrive home with the penitent bunch of chrysanthemums.

Detective Sergeant Christopher Rushton was prim. That is an adjective not appropriate for many policemen, but for him it was undoubtedly accurate. Primness did not prevent him being an effective officer. Indeed, in an era when too many policemen were busy cutting corners, his primness often manifested itself as a virtue. Chris played things by the book. If there was a rule, however obscure, he knew about it. Officers at the crime-face find red tape frustrating, and Chris made sure that others as well as himself did not end up in its coils. He was conscientious, and he knew his way round the police system. Although imagination might not be his strong suit, he was intelligent, and he had made himself something of an expert in the labyrinth of criminal law. His combination of qualities was a recipe for success in the modern police force, and in due course he would become a superintendent.

Chris knew that himself. He might not have old John Lambert's famed insights, but when his turn came he knew that he would direct his investigations competently enough to win his share of commendations. Not in Lambert's eccentric and outdated way, chasing across town and countryside like a young detective sergeant, but conventionally, from his office in the CID section.

He looked forward to directing his own team. It was one of the reasons why he had not once considered leaving the force, even when it had cost him his marriage. But perhaps Anne would have left him anyway: he was clear-sighted enough to realise that the job was sometimes no more than a convenient excuse for fractured relationships, that his wife might merely have tired of the dullness which he recognised in himself in his darker moments.

Tonight Chris wondered for the twentieth time why he had

let himself get involved in a ridiculous and perhaps ultimately dangerous charade. For a man whose watchword was reliability, this was not the right career move. The image of that magic word 'versatility' appearing on his file had beguiled him and betrayed him. He was going out to meet a woman, in the call of duty. With a wad of police money in his pocket, two hundred pounds to be spent 'only if necessary' on this most dubious of expenses.

Because he was prim, the irony and the humour of the enterprise did not strike him, though he realised now that Lambert and bloody Bert Hook were making the most of the situation. He was merely nervous, wondering if he could carry off the most bizarre role the CID had ever demanded of him, wondering how he should present himself for this strangest of all his working evenings.

He dressed himself as carefully as a woman on a first date and with as many changes of mind. In the end, he donned his best suit, the only one he had never used for plain-clothes work. It was dark blue, with the faintest of pinstripes in the light worsted cloth. His white shirt picked up the blue theme in its discreet striping; his tie had blue and silver stars in its rich crimson silk. New socks, the last in the drawer from Christmas, and black leather slip-on shoes with an elastic gusset, his only concession to 'casual' in his outfit. He polished the shoes vigorously to a high shine, as if trying to buff away even that tiny weakness.

He inspected himself again in the full-length mirror of the wardrobe. Not a policeman, he decided: that much was correct anyway. But as his confidence ebbed away at the thought of the night before him, he thought he looked too much like a tailor's dummy. He went downstairs into the kitchen and added the last, dubious touch to his outfit, the detail the woman had insisted upon when she set up this meeting, the thing which seemed to tip the whole business over into caricature.

Before he pinned the pink carnation to his lapel, he sniffed it automatically. It had no scent that he could detect, though he fancied he could smell his own nervousness upon his knuckles.

When Robert Watts finally came home in the evening, he had an unpleasant surprise. There was a car in the drive, and two senior policemen waiting to see him.

He took them reluctantly into the house. It was dark now, but there was no knowing how long they had been waiting for him, with curious neighbours conjecturing about the reason for their presence. "Well? What is it now?" he said aggressively. "I'm ready for a rest after a hard day's work, not a session with nosy bleeding pigs!"

Hook considered the florid, surly face unhurriedly. "You might be well advised to keep a civil tongue in your head, Mr Watts. Especially if you intend to sign on tomorrow as usual and collect your Giro."

It wasn't what they were there to pursue, of course, but it cowed him, took the edge off his aggression. He muttered a little to himself. Lambert waited for it to subside before he said, "Where have you been for the last two days, Mr Watts?"

"What's that to you? I don't see why—"

"You were asked to leave an address if you went away from home. You chose to ignore that."

The eyes which glared at them were bloodshot. Their experienced assessment divined a heavy night of drinking, followed by a day working off the hangover. A strong man this, but you couldn't get away with that kind of life for ever; he looked nearer to fifty than the forty-one they had recorded as his age. "I been 'elping a mate put new windows in. Took us the weekend and today."

"We may need details of where you were in due course. Or we may not, if you cooperate fully with us. Here or at the station, as you prefer."

"I've nothing to tell you. You've 'ad all I got to say." He tried to spit defiance at them, but it was no more than a ritual enmity now. He was physically exhausted, and they held all the cards. Lambert said, "You chose not to attend the inquest on Alison today."

"No. Was I supposed to? No one told *me* I was supposed to be there."

"It wasn't necessary, no. I just thought you might want to hear the evidence, such as it was."

"Well, I didn't, see? And I don't have to account for myself to the likes of you!"

"Not in that perhaps, but in other things you do, I'm glad to say. When did you begin abusing your daughter, Robert?"

120

The effect of this attack was remarkable. Watts, who had been standing in the middle of the room, fell back into the chair behind him as if he had been hit. They had been prepared for bluster, fury, perhaps even physical violence. Instead, Watts only said dully, "It wasn't like you think. Not abuse – I never thought of it as abuse."

"Not many people do at the time." Lambert sat down carefully on the edge of the settee, conscious of Hook cautiously following suit as they decided the man was not going to be violent. "It would be best if you gave us your side of it. The fuller you make it, the fewer the questions we shall need to ask." Interviews were a strange business, he thought: he felt himself moving in a few seconds from bully to therapist.

"Who told you?" said Watts. He ran a hand through hair that had probably not seen a comb that day. The smell of stale beer wafted from him across the patterned carpet.

"You know that we can't tell you that."

"Not Kate. She didn't know. I'm certain she didn't know." He shook his head, trying to clear his senses, like a boxer who has been heavily hit. It was important to him that Kate had never known of this shameful thing.

"How old was Alison when this began?"

He looked up at them, the bloodshot eyes widening. "Fifteen, I suppose, going on sixteen. There wasn't that much of it, you know."

"No, we don't, Robert. Not yet. We need you to tell us what happened."

Watts buried his head in his hands, pressing the palms in upon his temples, as if he sought to squeeze away these events from his brain. They could see a bald patch they had not noticed before amid the strands of unwashed grey hair. His voice was muffled as he spoke into his own chest. "I met her on the landing, one night when her mother was out. She was coming from the bathroom, in bra and pants. She said – she said, 'I'm getting to be a big girl now, aren't I, Robert?' It was the first time she'd ever called me by my name – I'd always been 'Dad' before. I didn't know what to make of that."

The moment was clearly still vivid for him, and he made it

121

vivid for them by his tortured intensity. He must have expected some sort of reaction. When none came, he slowly raised his head from the cradle of his arms and looked at them with those damaged, hunted eyes. "I followed her into her room. I don't know why – she just seemed to expect it. She stood in front of the full-length mirror in her wardrobe, holding her hands under her breasts, lifting them. Then she smiled and said, "I'll be a woman soon, won't I, Robert?" and I realised that she was watching me through the mirror."

Lambert said, "You were aware that she was a minor. That the law forbade you to have any sort of sexual relationship with her?"

"Yes. Yes, of course I was. But she looked so innocent, standing there in her white bra and her little white pants. I reached out to her and she put her arms round me. She said I was a real man, not like the boys she knew at school, that it was all right because there was no blood relationship between us. We held each other for a long time."

"And then you took it further."

"No. Not that first time, we didn't." He paused for a long moment, as if reluctant to relinquish the image of that first intimate exchange with his stepdaughter. Then he shook his head, so roughly that it seemed as if he was trying to punish himself. "But other times, in the months which followed, we did."

"There was full penetration and intercourse?"

"Yes. But only once. Most times I just ran my hands over her body, inside her clothes. She said she enjoyed it when we did it, wanted to do it again, but I wouldn't. I knew it was wrong, really. And I was scared rotten her mum would find out. Allie knew that – I think she was scared of her mum finding out, too, then, and that made her back off some of the times when she wanted to do it. She loved her mum, you see. And I did, too. Still do." He glanced up at them, then shrugged his big shoulders, a cornered bear, trapped by the intricacies of a life he could not fully understand.

"How long did these things go on, Robert?"

"Six months, I suppose. No longer. She said I was too inhibited, too conventional. Those were her words. She went on to other things."

122

He spoke wearily; they sensed in him an unexpected relief that this was out in the open at last. He was a man not fitted to keeping secrets, particularly ones like this. The two CID men studied him dispassionately: a rough-hewn man who resorted easily to violence, who had beaten his wife, who might have killed his daughter if she had threatened to reveal what he was now having to tell them himself. They only had his side of this squalid story, of course. All men said they were led on, whether they were or not. In this case, the details hardly mattered. What did was that this pathetic, dangerous hulk of a man had admitted a motive for killing the girl.

Lambert said, "Alison had a lot of money in the year before she died. Her clothes alone must have cost thousands."

He was planning to go on to ask Watts what he knew of his stepdaughter's activities at the weekends, but the man said unexpectedly, "You've found out about that, then." He shook his head hopelessly, too distraught now to register that they might not in fact have known what he was going to reveal. "She used what we had done against me. I suppose you know all about it. She said she needed money, but she wouldn't say what for. But she said she'd tell Kate about what we'd done, if I didn't help her."

"And how much did she have from you?"

He smiled bitterly at his own futility. "Whatever I had, she took. Thirty, forty, once fifty. I was working then, and whenever I was on overtime, she was there with her hand out as soon as Kate wasn't around. Kate thought I was betting it all away. That caused trouble, because I had to let her think that. I couldn't tell her where it was really going, could I?"

"How much did Alison have from you?"

"I don't know. I kept telling her it was the last time, that she could go and tell what she knew to anyone she fancied. But of course she came back again, and I couldn't let her tell Kate, could I? She must have had about three hundred, altogether."

Not enough to account for the wardrobe Alison Watts had assembled, let alone for the money they had now discovered in her building society account. But even if Robert Watts was lying, it seemed unlikely that he had earned enough to give her

123

much more than he admitted to. A resourceful and ruthless girl, this stepdaughter. Lambert said, "So she went on bleeding you, coming back for more, as blackmailers always do. You were desperate. There was only one way to stop her demands, and you took it."

He looked up at them again, the awful, bloodshot eyes full of fear and hostility. "No! No, I bloody didn't! You're trying to fit me up with this, aren't you, you bastards?"

A denial would have helped him, stoked his fury, but they did not give him one; instead, they studied his reactions to what had been suggested, dispassionately and cruelly. He had lifted his hands into the air in his excitement. After a moment, he dropped them back on to his knees, great helpless paws. He said hopelessly, "She stopped asking me for money in the last few months. She said once that she had bigger fish to fry now. And I liked her still, despite everything. She could be a little charmer, our Alison, when she wanted."

"Where were you on the Friday night when Alison disappeared, Robert?"

"I don't know. Why should I, at this length of time?"

"Because it would be useful to you to remember. If you had nothing to do with her death, that is."

"Well I can't. Maybe I was out having a drink. I usually am, on a Friday."

"It would pay you to recall the name of the pub, then. And to provide us with a witness to your presence there, if you can."

But none of them thought he was going to do that. They left him on the step of his empty, depressing house, scowling a ritual defiance at them as they drove away.

Chapter Fourteen

THERE was a cool edge now to the early autumn air. The mists dropped through the still night into the quiet Gloucestershire valleys. But in the towns the air was clear. And what that night might hold for the latest recruit to Cotswold Rendezvous was anyone's guess.

Christopher Rushton, alias Frank Lloyd, was glad of the cold: anything that would keep people off the streets of Cheltenham on this particular night was welcome to him. He looked anxiously to the left and the right as he took up his agreed station for the rendezvous, in the doorway of a clothes shop adjacent to the Odeon cinema. There was no sign of the woman yet. A female privilege to be late, he remembered. But surely any reasonable woman would realise that this was a nervous time for the man as well?

Within two minutes, he was shivering, resisting the temptation to stamp his feet to keep warm. He cursed the pink carnation. Not only did it seem absurdly festive in the darkness of this chill evening, but the agreement to display it meant that he could not wear a coat over his suit. No one seemed to be paying much attention to the lone man in the doorway; yet he felt very conspicuous, just when he wanted to remain anonymous to the citizens of this town, whose respectability was a national cliché.

Then, for the first time, he was noticed. He thrust his hands deep into his pockets, forcing himself to ignore the youth in the leather jacket who called over his shoulder to his companion to ask if 'Oscar Wilde' was waiting for him. The burst of raucous laughter which followed this sally almost brought out the policeman in him; deep in his pockets, his fingers itched to feel a collar, to show these yobs who really controlled this town. In his old, pre-CID days on the beat, these lads wouldn't have known what hit them. But Frank Lloyd wouldn't react like that, he told himself.

Staring resolutely through the plate-glass beside him, he pretended an absorbing interest in the unlined, robot faces of the dummies who carried the clothes. Their arms were held permanently at unlikely angles, their suits mirrored his own tailored rectitude. They seemed to be mocking him with their frozen smiles; for a fanciful moment, he expected their slim hands to gesture two-fingered contempt, their inscrutable faces to break into derisive smiles at his pretensions.

"Good evening."

He almost leapt out of his highly polished black casual shoes. The voice had a city accent. In his confusion, Chris could not place which city. A woman's voice, polite but confident. A voice which had done this before. He said, "Oh, good evening!" He almost added the 'madam' which would have completed his discomfort and given him away immediately as a policeman. "You must be . . ."

"Sharon. Well, Sherry to my friends." She looked him up and down; a slow, predatory smile gradually suffused her features. "And now my friends obviously include you, Mr Lloyd."

He managed a sickly smile. "Frank."

"Frank it is, then." She took his arm, turned him sideways into the street, walked his uncertain legs across the front of the cinema.

Chris tried in vain to think of something to say, failed, blurted out desperately, "That's nice!" Neither he nor she knew exactly what he was referring to, but she took it as evidence of good intent and gave his arm a reassuring squeeze.

She had a determined face, blue eyes which stared resolutely ahead, a smile which was now fixed and unmoving. Risking a glance down at the head beside him, Chris saw that the brass-blonde hair was darker at its roots. A bracelet heavy with gold charms glittered on the wrist which now lay firmly upon his forearm. The feet which marched so resolutely alongside his uncertain shoes were in high heels, the calves above them in sheer black nylon. Christopher Rushton had endured a conventional upbringing in a Methodist household: for him, black tights meant

126

loose women. It looked as though the deception of planting him at Cotswold Rendezvous was going to pay off, for this must surely be a tart. There might be kudos in this yet, if he could only carry it off.

They had to wait for the lights at the pedestrian crossing. She looked up appreciatively into his weakly smiling face and said, "Lucky old me, then!" Caught in the headlights of the car accelerating away from the lights, her top teeth were regular and very white. Too regular and too white, he decided. A dental plate, for sure. In his limited range of intimate exchanges with the opposite sex, he had never had to deal with one of those before.

But then he had never had to deal with a situation like this before. He knew he must take things far enough on to get the evidence they required and yet stop before he was fatally compromised. He wondered miserably when that point might be. Images of bedrooms and discarded clothing swam before him. As the panic welled within him, he wondered why he had ever let that smiling Machiavelli Lambert talk him into this.

He said desperately, "Where shall we go, Sherry?" He had to force out the name; his mouth clenched tight on it, as it done in anticipation of foul-tasting medicine when he was a child. "Should we take in a movie, do you think?" It seemed the right transatlantic idiom for this phoney situation, and he thought he trotted it out quite well.

And a film would give him a blessed period of silence, a time to re-group, to marshall his resources. Even to organise a disciplined retreat, if that should be necessary. At this moment, cutting this thing short seemed to him a most blissful prospect. A non-consummation devoutly to be wished. He would remember that phrase for Bert Hook – show him he wasn't the only one who could play with words.

Below him, the carefully made-up blue eyes looked up into his brown ones; the small, determined chin and the yellow curls shook dismissively; the bright red lips pursed – and shattered his new plans. "No, I don't think so, Frank. We need the chance to get to know each other, don't we?" The blue eyes widened interrogatively, moist and alluring. Then

127

the right one winked, suddenly and horribly, like that of a playful witch.

He was an emotional non-swimmer, with the current taking him out of his depth. He did not know how to resist it. "A drink?" he said desperately.

She giggled, then nestled expertly into the crook of his arm. "Oh, all right, then, cheeky. I know you're just trying to get a girl tipsy because you want to get her defences down. But we'll have a drink first, if you like."

There was a wealth of meaning in that word 'first', Chris thought miserably. A wealth he was more than ever certain he did not want to inherit.

They found a pub. Or rather Sherry did: it was obvious she had been there before. Rushton would have stayed in the brightly lit lounge beside the main bar, but while he ordered, she went and sat round the corner, where he discovered that there were a series of smaller and more private alcoves with tiny round tables.

He had half-expected her to order a port and lemon, as ladies of easy virtue had done in the films of his youth, but she had a gin and tonic, and then another and another, while he drank halves of lager. A pity, really, to be so modest when he was using the wedge of tenners the police had provided, but he needed to keep sober. Or fairly sober: he was aware of a need for Dutch courage which he had not felt so powerfully since he was a teenager, pretending to be at ease in situations which were completely new to him. Well, this was certainly one of those, he thought, as he pulled desperately at his third half.

She asked him about himself, and he went carefully but a little too rapidly through the persona they had prepared for Frank Lloyd. A sales manager, down here from the Midlands base of the company, geeing up the sales team in Herefordshire and Avon. Resident here for a few months; divorced; lonely; in search of a little excitement during the long winter nights. He had rehearsed this background so well that he came out with this last bit of it almost in those words, and Sherry laughed and said, "Cheeky! We shall have to see what we can do for poor, lonely Frank in due course, won't we?" She put her hand upon his knee, moved it up to his thigh, stroked it appreciatively but absently as she

128

considered the plasterwork of the high ceiling. He had to go for more drinks to break the contact.

He remembered to make the token enquiries about her situation. She said she was divorced but 'comfortable', living in her own flat in Cheltenham. Looking for a little excitement out of life. It scarcely mattered what background a tom was going to give herself, he thought, but for form's sake you had to ask. She worked as a secretary in a small supermarket, relaying the orders for supplies, she said. Fat chance, thought Chris. He wondered what her price would be, when it came to it, and whether you were supposed to bargain or just accept it. Well, that was one thing in which he would not need to take the initiative. Any self-respecting tom was going to want to fix the terms of the bargain before she got down to business.

She was not a bad sort, really, this Sherry. He would want to let her down lightly, when the time came. She was just a pawn in the game. Getting at the men who were organising this racket was what they were after, and he would make that clear to her. Nothing personal. No hard feelings. An unfortunate phrase that: he giggled a little to himself at the private joke.

He was able to do so without the fear of discovery because Sherry was away at the bar. She had insisted on buying her own round; she wasn't a bad sort at all, really. It should have sounded a warning bell in his innocent, drink-stumbling brain, but it didn't. And she brought him back a pint, not a half: business must be good in her dubious trade.

He reeled a little when they went out into the cool night air. She put her arm round his waist and said, "Steady, Frank!" and he wondered for a moment quite who Frank was.

Then he straightened and said austerely "Quite right!" and concentrated on walking at his full height and very straight. She seemed to find this amusing, and they giggled together. An officer on the beat regarded them suspiciously whilst they walked past the brightly lit shop windows, and Chris had to resist the temptation to tell the young constable exactly who he really was.

The flat was on the ground floor of a quiet block. Chris tried to assess the surroundings, to decide whether the man who had set her up here owned more apartments in the same block, where

129

other prostitutes might at this very moment be entertaining other clients, but it was too dark for him to see much. And his brain seemed to be refusing to work with its normal efficiency. Hurst the Worst, that was the bloke they were hoping was behind this lot, he remembered. He hoped he was: it wouldn't do DI Rushton's promotion prospects any harm if they netted a big one like Hurst. It was as well to remind himself of his real purpose here; he had almost got used to being Frank Lloyd now, and it was really quite agreeable to have his arm round this warm, soft female form.

It was a much nicer flat inside than he had been expecting. Spacious, with thick carpeting and a Persian rug, and the light coming not from the ceiling but from lamps on two small tables on either side of the marble fireplace. Sherry switched on the living flame gas fire and he slumped rather too heavily on to the low, soft settee in front of it. She reached down towards him with both hands and he thought the moment had come. But she merely unpinned the carnation he had long since forgotten and smoothed its ruffled petals. "I'll just put this in water," she said. "Shame to waste it."

He went to the bathroom and relieved himself of a surprising quantity of lager, resting his forehead on the wall above the lavatory as he did so, directing the copious flow with elaborate care into the bowl, making sure he did not defile this agreeably female retreat. He spent a long time washing his hands, then looked slyly into the medicine cabinet, to see if the condoms which he knew must appear at some point were in there. There was no sign of them. "Find the johnny!" he whispered to himself, then giggled inordinately at what suddenly seemed a highly humorous thought.

By the time he returned to the lounge, Sherry had set a pot of coffee on the low table beside the settee and come to sit beside him. "I think you need this, Frank," she said, not unkindly.

The golden-hearted tart, he thought – it wasn't just a myth. "Very good of you," he said. "But I'm not drunk, you know." She smiled, he sniggered, and then both of them suddenly found it very funny, so that they laughed out loud together, for what seemed quite a long time.

When they finished, he had his jacket off, and she had drawn her knees up on to the seat of the sofa beside him. The black nylon was stretched now, and there was much of it to see, because there was an awful lot of Sherry's thigh pressing against his. He put his hand on her calf as she slid her fingers through the gap on his shirt, where a button had mysteriously undone itself. His hand slid up over her darkly glistening knee to the soft area of her thigh as she kissed him, exploring his teeth with the tip of her tongue. Nothing at Central Methodist Sunday School had prepared him for this.

She had a bra which he would never be able to unfasten, but that didn't worry him. She'd help him when the time came, he was confident of that. He shifted his position, lifted the compliant body a little, stroked a rounded buttock beneath the tights. He was really quite good at this, after all. He smelt an intoxicating mixture of powder, perfume and deodorant, and she breathed "Oh, Frank!" softly into his ear. This bloody Frank had it all going for him, he thought. Better than being a bloody policeman, any day.

It was the moment of truth, the moment which recalled him belatedly to his duty. Something was wrong here. She was being very kind to him, helping him along in a situation which was new to him, and he was grateful to her for her sensitivity. But they had never fixed a price, and they should surely have agreed one by now. It was all very high-class, this. An awful fear seized him that the police funds in his pocket might after all be insufficient, that he might not have enough money with him with him. Be just like John Bloody Lambert to leave him short.

He struggled to get his face free of that bewitching mass of blonde hair. "Just a minute, Sherry," he said firmly into her small ear.

She sighed. "The boys' room is it again, Frank? Well. I'm not surprised. But don't be too long, now you've got me interested." She moved away and poured herself another cup of the now lukewarm coffee.

"No. I don't need to go." Suddenly he did, but that would have to wait. He tried to distance himself, to sound experienced and official. "We haven't fixed a fee, Sherry," he said. He fumbled towards his hip pocket for his wallet and the wedge. "It's very good of you to be so trusting and to take so much trouble over me, of course, but I really think we ought to—"

The slap was so hard that his face was still tingling an hour later. "What the damned bloody buggering hell do you think you're about?" she said furiously.

She did not wait for a reply. It was just as well it was a ground floor flat. She might well have flung him down the stairs if there had been any. In less than thirty seconds, he was out on the street in his shirt sleeves, trying hard to button the belt on his trousers, holding his jacket clumsily under one arm. There was no chance to offer the kind, infuriated lady any sort of explanation.

The taxi driver did not want to take him. The smell of drink, the dribble of blood from the nostril, the jacket only covering one arm on a cold night, were all ominous signs to his experienced eye. Rushton had to show him his warrant card to prevent him driving off. And when he made him stop halfway home so that he could disappear behind a hedge to empty his straining bladder, he found that the flies of his best suit were still wide open.

It was not a dignified way for a detective inspector to spend an evening.

Chapter Fifteen

THE headmaster of Oldford Comprehensive school arrived at work very early on the morning of Tuesday, 19 October. Normally he would have been happy to be noted showing such devotion to duty, but on this particular morning Thomas Murray, MA (Birmingham), FRSA, moved through the familiar corridors of his school furtively.

He met his caretaker, George Phillips, and reflected that this man, so elusive when there was hard work to be undertaken, seemed always to be present where he was least wanted. Phillips rattled his mop and bucket ostentatiously and tugged at an imaginary cap in hollow deference. He plainly wondered why the head had arrived before eight. Tom gave him no satisfaction on that. He afforded him the briefest of greetings and stood in the corridor until the man shuffled away.

He waited until Phillips was safely behind the door of one of the science labs before he hastened down the corridor and turned towards the school library. The door was locked, but he had his key at the ready. He found the files of newspapers readily enough. *The Times* was now recorded on microfiche, but he was happy to see that the well-thumbed copies of the *Gloucester Citizen* had not succumbed to modern technology but were kept in an uneven pile on the bottom shelf of the reference section.

The room seemed unnaturally quiet. The pages of newsprint rustled loud as he searched anxiously for the relevant copy. It was there: Friday, 23 July. He sought out the entertainments section and breathed a sigh of relief. One of the films at the multiplex cinema in Gloucester had been *The English Patient*. He had seen it, with his wife, though not of course on the twenty-third of July. But the police wouldn't know that, and if they asked questions, both he and Ros would be able to tell them about the film.

He locked up the library and went back to his headmaster's office with a lighter heart. He only needed Ros to back him up now. She'd not been as compliant as usual lately. But surely, when he convinced her of the importance of it, she would tell this one small lie for him.

DI Chris Rushton took care to be at work at the normal time on that morning. His head ached and his mouth was dry; when he inspected himself in the mirror in the locker room at Oldford CID, he looked unusually pale. But he was there, his shirt and tie as immaculate as usual. At least that would ensure that there could be no cheap jibes from Superintendent Lambert and Sergeant Bloody Hook about the effects on punctuality of a dissolute evening.

He reported to them when they came in for the meeting they had arranged. He spoke as coldly, as neutrally, as he could of the blank he had drawn in the guise of Frank Lloyd, watching suspiciously for any signs of amusement in his listeners. "There's no need to spend any more time over Cotswold Rendezvous," he concluded. "The lady I met was a perfectly genuine member of a singles club."

"Disappointing, that. Just looking for companionship, I suppose," said Lambert innocently.

"Well, yes, sir. How much more than that, I couldn't of course say."

"No, of course you couldn't, Chris. As you were operating only in the line of duty."

"There was no hint of anything other than a woman looking innocently for some sort of relationship. Once I had established that, I got out of the situation as quickly as I could, naturally." Chris tried not to think of that picture of himself with shirt and flies undone and jacket under his arm on the respectable Cheltenham street.

But Bert Hook had noted his unease. "Naturally, yes. Er – at what point exactly did you decide that the lady was genuine and not a hooker, Chris?"

"That I don't propose to tell you. It was an embarrassing enough assignment you landed me with, I can tell you. And if—"

"Get as far as drawers off, did we?"

"Of course we didn't! I merely established that the lady was genuine rather than a tom, and then got out with what dignity I could. Without blowing my cover, of course." He turned back to Lambert. "And I think I should say here and now, sir, that I didn't find this assignment easy. I think I should point out that I do not feel that undercover work is one of my strengths. You may wish to bear this in mind if any future plans to infiltrate officers into situations like this are envisaged."

There. He had got it out, the statement he had prepared for himself as he drove in to Oldford nick that morning. He wasn't going to endure anything like last night again. He said stiffly, "Anyway, it looks as though we have to eliminate Eddy Hurst from any connection with this."

Lambert nodded regretfully. "I'd still like to know where Alison Watts went at the weekends, though. She was pulling in plenty of money from somewhere over those last months."

Hook said, "Some of it came from her stepfather. Could she have been blackmailing other people as well?"

"I certainly wouldn't put it past her. Once she had found it so easy to get money from Robert Watts in that way, she might have been tempted to look for other victims. Blackmailers often do. It's when they turn the screw too tight that they become murder victims."

"Who else did she have a hold on? Jamie Allen?"

"Scarcely. They were just boy- and girlfriend, quite openly. Nothing illicit that we know of in their relationship which had to be concealed. In any case, Jamie hasn't any substantial funds of his own, and that formidable mother of his would have given short shrift to Alison Watts if she'd tried to get money out of her."

"Likewise Barbara Bullimore to anyone trying to make money out of her brother's association with Alison. A formidable female, that one." Bert Hook shuddered reminiscently. He was an expert on iron women in authority from the Barnardo's days of his youth. When he spoke of formidable females, people deferred to his expertise. No one who had met Barbara Bullimore, whether

135

socially or behind her library counter, would have demurred from Bert's view.

Lambert said, "But Jason Bullimore certainly had something to hide, especially with his past record of susceptibility to forbidden young schoolgirl flesh. It's worth checking out whether Alison tried to get money out of him after she'd ended their relationship. But I can't see that he would be able to provide the amount of money Alison was spending in those last months – not unless he had more than a schoolteacher's salary to draw on. In view of the value of the clothes the SOCO team brought in from her room and what her peers have told us about her sudden affluence, we've trawled the banks and building societies for information. It turns out that Alison had an account with the Cheltenham and Gloucester."

"And is there much in it?" said Hook.

"Just over two thousand pounds. With considerable credits and debits over the last few months. Presumably the debits are largely explained by those clothes and shoes. By the way, we haven't as yet found the pass-book for this account."

Rushton said, "It could still be a crime of passion. Both Jamie Allen and Jason Bullimore were disappointed lovers. In different ways." As the two experienced faces looked into his, he felt himself blushing at the memory of his own amorous fiasco ten hours previously. Telling himself sternly that these two grinning faces could not possibly know of that debacle, he went on determinedly, "Jamie was certainly still very smitten with her, but being kept at arm's length in the months before she died. And from what you say, I gather that Jason Bullimore might still have been emotionally involved with her at the time of her death. Whether he loved or hated her, he could still have been driven to kill her."

"True." Lambert wondered exactly what had happened to the old Puritan Rushton last night: it was not usual for him to speculate like this about emotional matters. "Are we any nearer to establishing a time of death?"

Rushton shook his head. "Only in a negative way. I've collated all the door-to-door and other information on the computer. We haven't turned up anyone who saw Alison Watts later than five o'clock on the evening of Friday the twenty-third of July. Of course, she might have moved out of the area altogether when she disappeared. But we know that her body was put into the Wye in this area eventually, so she was almost certainly killed somewhere round here. Everything points to the fact that she died shortly after she was last seen. It could have been a woman, of course. A ligature was used, and it bit into the front of her neck, so she was almost certainly attacked from behind. It didn't require great strength. But equally, she might have been killed by someone we haven't even located yet."

Hook said, "Meantime, we have to concentrate on the candidates we have. Robert Watts, Jamie Allen, Jason Bullimore. Three likely lads."

Lambert nodded. "Plus an outsider coming up on the rails. Thomas Murray, headmaster and devious bugger. He's hiding something, but as yet I'm not quite sure what."

However diligent a police investigation, however extensive the team, chance plays more part than the public think. Especially when a crime has been committed well before the enquiry begins, a lucky break is often necessary to trigger a successful outcome. They had such a break later that day. It came from an unlikely source, but it was just the sort of information which seemed likely to be highly significant. It proved that one at least of the people who had been closest to Alison Watts had lied to them in his statement.

At three o'clock, Margaret Peplow, Director of Sixth Form Studies at Oldford Comprehensive, rang in to the station and asked to speak to Superintendent Lambert in the CID section. She came straight to the point when she was put through. "One of the girls who spoke to you in the group last week has come up with new information."

"We shall need to speak to her face to face, Mrs Peplow. We can't take anything on hearsay in a murder investigation."

"Of course. But I'd rather you didn't come into the school, if it could be avoided. There's enough speculation going on here, as you can imagine, without it being fuelled by another visit from

137

your team. I'll bring the girl in after school, if that's acceptable. Say in an hour from now?"

"Yes. That would be ideal. And stay with the girl while we question her, if you're willing to do that. It might be helpful."

And it would let a sensible woman see that they didn't use the third degree methods on adolescents of which they were so often accused.

"Fine. Thank you. She's a reliable girl, Jane. I'd be pretty certain what she tells you will be true."

When they arrived, an hour later to the minute, Lambert immediately recognised the dark-haired girl who had been their main source of information during their initial meeting with the group of sixth form girls at the school. Jane Harvey looked a little overawed by the police machine and the fact that she was now to be interviewed with Mrs Peplow sitting alongside her. But she was observant, intelligent, composed, considering her age and the circumstances of this meeting. Lambert, anxious this time to have the full truth as she saw it, decided that it would do no harm to ruffle her a little.

"You said that you were not aware of any association between Alison and an older man. That wasn't quite true, was it, Jane? You were quite aware that Alison had had an affair with Mr Bullimore, who taught her English, but you chose not to reveal that to us."

The two female faces were both startled. Margaret Peplow was going to speak, but before she could do so, Jane Harvey said quickly, "You asked us about the months before Alison's death. Whether she had any connections with older men in those months. I said I didn't know of anything which happened then. Her relationship with – with Mr Bullimore had ended before that."

It was casuistry, and she knew it. Lambert let it go. "All right, Jane. I think you know you should have told us, but you had a mistaken sense of loyalty. Incidentally, you will notice we haven't arrested Mr Bullimore, so the connection didn't automatically mean that we thought we had our murderer. It would have been better if you'd told us, wouldn't it?"

"Yes. I suppose so."

"I can assure you it would. Because this is a murder enquiry, and we were always going to find out things like that. So what is it that you have to tell us now, Jane?"

"A small thing. It's probably not important. But Mrs Peplow thought you should know about it."

"Quite possibly both of you are right, Jane. We have a whole multitude of facts about Alison and the people she knew on record now. And we shall have many more before the case is solved. Most of them are bound to be unimportant, eventually: you're right about that. But we don't know which ones at this stage. So Mrs Peplow is right, too. We have to know. What is it you have to tell us?"

"It's Jamie. Jamie Allen. Alison's boyfriend."

"Yes, we know Jamie Allen."

"Well, I'm sure it doesn't mean anything. But I know he told you he didn't see Alison after we all left school at lunch-time on that Friday at the end of the summer term. We've talked, you see, at the school, all of us, this last few days."

Lambert smiled at her. "I'm sure you have, Jane. It probably seems as though you've talked of nothing else. But what is it you have to tell us about Jamie?"

"Only – well, he did see her again after that. He saw her that Friday evening. As a matter of fact, I think they had a blazing row."

Christopher Rushton was tired but happy. Well, 'relieved' might be a better word, he thought. He'd got through the day all right, and Clever Bastard Lambert and Sarcy Bugger Hook hadn't been able to break him down, or find out any of the details of what had happened last night. He'd even managed to hint to Lambert as he left that this had been a job well done, that although the results had been negative, DI Rushton had displayed resource and insight in an undercover role that went beyond the call of duty.

Had even displayed, in fact, a hitherto unsuspected versatility. That magic word might after all now appear on his file. John Lambert might have a warped sense of humour at times, but he was fair, and he had a reputation for looking after his staff.

And now Chris could relax at last in his empty, tidy house. He went and helped himself to one of the cans of bitter which had lain undisturbed in the fridge for months. A modest celebration seemed in order. He was so exhausted that he suspected he might eventually fall asleep in front of the television, but that wouldn't matter. For almost the first time since Anne had left him, the house seemed a private haven he was glad to reach, instead of a lonely, sterile place. He deserved a rest, after what he had been through in the last twenty-four hours. Thank God it was all over, without any real damage done.

The telephone rang several times before its insistent note pierced his slumber. He looked hastily at his watch as he stumbled into the hall, kicking over the empty can beside his armchair. Half past eight already: he must have been asleep for over an hour. He blurted the number automatically into the mouthpiece as he snatched up the phone.

"Mr Lloyd. I thought you weren't there."

A female voice, cool and businesslike. He almost said it had got a wrong number. Then he remembered last night, and horror flooded into his head. "Who – who is that? If it's Sherry, I'm terribly sorry, but it was all an awful misunderstanding. I can only—"

"Relax, Mr Lloyd. Frank, isn't it? This isn't Sharon, or Sherry, as I think she's known to her intimates. I expect you're pleased about that, Frank."

"Look, who is this? I don't—"

"We heard about your little misunderstanding with Sharon, Frank. We've smoothed her down for you. Put her in touch with what we think might be a more appropriate gentleman. Less – well, let's just say less ardent than you, Frank."

"Look, unless you tell me who you are and what this is about, I shall ring off." But he knew by now that he wouldn't, even as his mind struggled to focus. There was a tap on his phone. Priority. By now, the call would be being traced. He must keep this mysterious woman talking.

"All in good time, Frank. I wouldn't ring off, though. That might not be to your advantage."

The silky voice took on menace in the last phrase. And Rushton, disconcerted as he was, was enough of a policeman to scent something evil at the other end of the phone. "What is it that you want with me?"

"We'd like to supply your needs, Frank, that's all. At a price."

"What sort of price?" Rushton tried desperately to think not as a CID man but as Frank Lloyd, Sales Director in search of sexual excitement.

"That's more like it, Frank. Interested, are we?"

"I suppose I might be, if the price was right."

"Ah! Now, you sell things yourself, Frank, so you know that the kind of thing you seem to be after doesn't come cheap. Not if the quality is high. And I can tell you that the standard of the goods we are offering is of the highest quality. 'Attractive female company, with no holds barred,' you said you wanted, in your application to Cotswold Rendezvous. Well, for the right people, there needn't be any holds barred. But we're talking big bucks, Frank. Big bucks and young, pretty girls. Unsoiled goods, you might say. The very best. For those who can pay for the very best. Interested?"

"I said I was, didn't I? But I'd need more details."

"All in good time, Frank. It's got to be discreet, this. We don't want the law cutting in on us, do we? Restrictive, lawyers are, when it comes to sexual services. Some of the things we can offer, they don't approve of, if you take my meaning." The female voice was as silky as ever, but it sounded older now. "What we like to do is to establish exactly what our clients would like in the way of sexual services, and then see if we can provide it for them. And Frank, just to excite you, I have to tell you that we can usually supply what the client wants. If he wants it badly enough to pay the rate."

"I can pay, if I get what I want." Chris was surprised how assertive his voice was, how easily he had dropped into the personality this seemed to require.

"I'm glad to hear that, Mr Lloyd. We'll need to process your application, discuss terms. Discreetly, of course. That's in the interests of both sides."

"Yes. I would certainly want any involvement on my part to remain private."

"Good. We can assure you of our discretion. We provide certain other supplies as well as sexual ones. Supply certain substances which the lawyers also don't approve of. Some of our clients feel that is a valuable service. But all that can be discussed later, when we have assured ourselves that you have the means to proceed with your little project."

"And when I have seen the quality of what you have to offer."

"Quite. You sound like a man with whom we could do business, Mr Lloyd."

With whom. For a moment, he wanted to laugh at the precision of her grammar, in the light of what she was offering him. That showed how strongly the adrenalin was flowing, how careful he must be. He had better cut this as short as he could, if he was not to make some sort of mistake. "I hope so. Because you sound as if you can supply what I am looking for."

"I'm sure we can." With the fish securely hooked, she too wanted to finish the conversation now. He might start wanting more information if she gave him time to think, and there was no way she would give him that. Better to finish this while his senses were still reeling with the heady prospects of sex. "Pretty young girls, for a start, Mr Lloyd. Untarnished goods. I think I sense from talking to you that you could be in the market for them."

She was pleased with that; his breathy, eager reaction showed that she had guessed right about his preferences. She gave him the address he should attend if he wanted to take this further, the name of the man he should ask for. Then she put down the phone and entered the name Frank Lloyd on her list of 'Potential Clients'. Another rich sucker in tow. What gullible fools men in search of sexual excitement were!

Mr Hurst would be pleased with her efforts.

Chapter Sixteen

HOOK rang Jamie Allen's house at eight in the morning on Wednesday, 20 October, to say they were coming to see him. It put that formidable mother on her guard, but it was better to confront the redoubtable Mrs Allen than to see Jamie at school, with all the attention that would bring.

Lambert was in no mood to waste time. He tackled the boy head on, in front of his mother. "You lied to us, Jamie. Wasting police time is a serious offence. Especially when a murder is being investigated. And it won't benefit anyone, least of all yourself. We're now asking ourselves why you chose to deceive us when we first came to see you."

They were sitting on upright chairs in the dining room of the Edwardian house. There was a musty smell on this cool autumn morning. Jamie sat with his mother on one side of the heavy mahogany dining table. The boy was pale, the length of his thin neck accentuated by the T-shirt he had chosen to put on when he took off his school shirt. Perhaps he had intended to look relaxed; instead, the shirt, with its message about protecting badgers, merely made him look vulnerable. His pale arms stuck out like those of a pipe cleaner figure; he eased his elbows on to the edge of the table to imply relaxation, but it looked a stiff, awkward movement.

His mother glanced sideways at her son. She had dressed for this occasion in the half hour since Hook's phone call had caught her preparing breakfast in her house-coat. Over-dressed, some would say, for this time in the morning. She wore a deep maroon dress with a necklace of small rubies. A dark red comb was precisely placed in the middle of her thick head of hair, restricting any tendency the hair might have to move if she became agitated. A gold bangle gleamed softly on her wrist. She was dressed for some

143

elegant but sombre social occasion, not for this sordid exposure of her son's evasions.

Lambert remembered being taken by his own mother to stand outside the high, studded doors of Wormwood Scrubs in the early 'sixties. He could not have been more than fourteen. It was when he had first said he wanted to become a policeman, and his appalled parent had taken him to watch a mother's last visit to the son who was to be hanged in the morning. That working-class woman had dressed in her best clothes, had come to the prison in a long, dark dress and a hat which might have been more suitable for a wedding than for this last, hopeless meeting. Lambert had had no idea what effect his mother had intended, but the incident had not put him off a police career. Rather had he been fascinated with the awful melodrama of that morning, of the man he would never see who was about to be executed, and the tragic, doomed elegance of the grey-haired, erect woman in the dark dress, moving in patient silence to the last meeting with her son.

Mrs Allen's son could not be hanged, whatever he had done to the girl who had rejected him. But his suffering mother seemed to have dressed for a wake, to have acquired the same awful dignity as that other woman from all those years ago. She said softly, "You had better tell the Superintendent what he wants to know, James. The whole truth, this time."

This time Jamie made no attempt to exclude her from the interview. Perhaps he was glad of whatever support he could get in this room where his lying was about to be exposed. Perhaps, thought Bert Hook as he turned to a new page of his notebook, they were moving swiftly to the last act of this drama, and the boy expected to be taken out to the police car and driven away from his family at the end of it.

Jamie suddenly shivered. His T-shirt was woefully inadequate for this musty, cold room. He said, "What I told you about Allie and me is true. We were very close, closer than anyone else knew. We'd have got back together all right, if – if . . ."

Suddenly he was in tears, and the mother who had so hated his liaison with the dead girl moved her hand along the table to clasp his unresisting fist. Lambert and Hook watched the pair dispassionately, almost cruelly, for a long moment. Then

Lambert said, "That may be, Jamie. But you lied to us. Lied to us about the most important thing of all. The time when you last saw Alison Watts."

Jamie nodded sharply, almost eagerly. He drew a long, shuddering breath, composing himself to speak evenly. "I'm not quite sure what I said about that, Mr Lambert."

The title came oddly, reminding them of this lad's determinedly respectable upbringing, of the shame and agony that his arrest and trial could bring to this house. "I think you do remember what you told us, Jamie. But I'll remind you. When asked about your last contact with a murder victim, you said that you didn't see Alison Watts after midday on Friday the twenty-third of July. We now know that that wasn't correct. As you knew it wasn't at the time you told us."

Jamie glanced sideways at his mother, whose face seemed to have turned to stone. He now seemed happy to have the woman whom he had so furiously rejected from their first meeting in this house sitting at his side. Hook, preparing to record a new version in his notebook, wondered what had passed between the pair in the three days since they had last been here. Jamie said abruptly, "You're right. I did see Allie again that day. In the evening."

"At what point in the evening?"

"Early. Before six o'clock. I went round to see her at her house. We went out for a walk so that we could talk."

"So when was your last sight of Alison?"

"About six-thirty."

"Right. So the next question we have to ask is why didn't you tell us this five days ago?"

"I – I suppose I thought it wouldn't reflect very well on me, in your eyes." He glanced sideways at the still, silent figure of his mother. "And I didn't want it recorded that my final words with Allie had been spoken in anger." He blurted out the last phrase, close to a renewed descent into tears. They watched the mother's fingers tightening white over what suddenly seemed the small and childishly vulnerable fist of her son.

"You had a row with Alison Watts, didn't you, Jamie, on that last Friday evening? What was it about?"

"About us. About the future we should have had together."

145

For the first time, Lambert glanced at Mrs Allen, and the lady who had been so uncharacteristically restrained took it as her cue to speak. "They need something a little more specific than that, Jamie. You'll have to tell them what you were arguing about." She looked at the bent head beside her.

A long, shuddering breath again, as the boy fought for a control that was physically painful for him. He spoke eventually, in a quiet monotone which masked the emotion beneath. "She told me she wanted to finish with me. That we hadn't got a future together. I said we had."

"I see. But something must have provoked this discussion of your own relationship. What was it, Jamie?"

Jamie Allen glanced up at Lambert, as if surprised that he could be so perceptive. In fact, Jamie was wondering how much they had been told already. But no one could have known what had passed between him and Allie on that last night. He had spoken of it to no one, until now. "I didn't want her to keep going into Cheltenham, at the weekends. On Friday and Saturday nights."

"But she wouldn't listen to you, would she?"

"No."

"Where did she go to, Jamie, on those weekend trips? Those trips which were so painful to you."

"I don't know. She wouldn't tell me. Even then, that last time, she wouldn't tell me. We had a blazing row, you know." He looked up at them, as if it might be a surprise to them, as if even now it was a surprise to him.

Lambert nodded. "You've no idea what she got up to in Cheltenham? Or Gloucester?" Those historic and respectable towns suddenly sounded in his ears like Sodom and Gomorrah. In another context, he would have allowed himself to laugh.

Fortunately for the reputation of Oldford CID, Jamie Allen replied quickly. "No. She wouldn't ever tell me. But it was lucrative. She had lots of money to throw about in those last months."

"Yes. We've found that out for ourselves, Jamie. It would have been helpful if you'd revealed it to us earlier."

He nodded, then anticipated their next question. "I don't know where the money came from, you know. I didn't really press her about that."

Perhaps he hadn't wanted to hear the truth. Lambert said, "Do you think she was involved in any way with the sale of illicit substances, Jamie?"

"No." He seemed almost disappointed, as if he would have preferred that solution to things which were even less agreeable for him to confront.

"Did you ever see Alison using drugs? Hard or soft?"

"No." He glanced quickly at his mother beside him. "One or two people in the school have had cannabis once or twice. I've never seen anything worse. But Allie never bothered with it; she said she thought it was stupid."

"And yet she was getting money from somewhere. Big money. How do you account for that, Jamie?"

There was one other obvious source of such pickings for an attractive young girl, and it was in the minds of all four people gathered around the dark table in that quiet room. But the young man at the centre of the tableau produced a different suggestion, an ugly slur upon his dead lover, but perhaps more acceptable to him than the more obvious one. "I don't really know why Allie was suddenly so rich. But I think she might have been getting money from people because – well, because of things she knew about them."

Lambert and Hook heard the sharp, involuntary snatch of breath from the woman at the boy's side, even as they kept their eyes steadily on Jamie Allen's face. The Superintendent said calmly, "Blackmail, you mean? It's as well to give things their proper name, you know."

The young face was wide-eyed, wanting to deny it, knowing well that it couldn't. "I suppose so, yes. I don't think Allie thought of it as that, but it was. I told her so. That was another thing we rowed about, that last night, as well as her weekend activities. She just said she was taking money wherever she found it, from people who could well afford to subsidise her."

"And who were these people, Jamie?"

"I don't know." He stared miserably at the table.

They all realised that he did know, that he had a name or names to give them. It was his mother, who had been so quiet through all of this, who now said, "I think you do know, Jamie. And you had much better tell the officers now than try to conceal it."

147

Jamie glanced at her sharply, then transferred his gaze miserably back to Lambert. They all knew he was going to tell them, that the respect for authority so deeply embedded in his upbringing would not let him turn stubborn on them now, when he had gone so far. The CID men wondered if he was going to tell them what they already knew, that Alison Watts had extracted money from her stepfather with the threat to tell her mother the details of how he had abused her. Detection was in their blood after all these years, so that each of them found himself hoping that this would be some new name, some other man or woman with a reason to have killed this troublesome young chancer of a girl.

In a voice they could only just hear even in that quiet room, Jamie said, "I don't like this. Can you promise me that what I have to tell you won't go any further?"

"You know we can't do that, Jamie. The most we can say is that we shall treat your information with discretion. If it has a bearing on a murder trial, it may even have to come out in court. If it doesn't, it probably won't go any further than this."

The boy nodded bleakly. The conventions of school as well as home were strong in him. You did not 'snitch' on your mates. Or even on your teachers. But now he must. "It was Mr Bullimore," he said reluctantly. "Allie had gone to bed with him, at one time. And she said she was going to get money out of him, by threatening to tell other people about it. We had a fierce set-to about it, on that Friday night, but she wouldn't listen to me. I think she went off to see Mr Bullimore when she left me."

Tom Murray could feel the beginnings of sweat on his palms. He knew he must keep his voice even and light, must show no sign of his anger. "I think you're getting this rather out of proportion, Ros," he said. "It's no big deal, really. I'm just asking you to—"

"If it's no big deal, let's leave it," said Ros. "I don't fancy telling lies. Anyway, I'm no good at it, never have been. I'd only let you down." Her lips turned up at the corners into a small, unconscious smile, which looked to Tom to be a deliberate mockery of his concern. It seemed to say to him, "I have no need to concern myself with dishonesty; more fool you if you are not as stainless as me."

He tried again, forcing himself into a broader smile than hers.

"You'll just have to trust me, old girl." He patted her bottom lightly, affectionately, experimentally.

She rounded upon him, so suddenly that he was thoroughly taken aback. "I'm not your 'old girl'!" she said furiously. "And I *won't* have to trust you. Why should I? When you don't trust me with anything. Not even with the reason why you want me to lie to the police for you."

"It probably won't come to that," he said desperately, "and all I'm saying is that if it did—"

"If it did, you want me to tell deliberate lies! And to policemen who are looking for a murderer! For no reason. Or rather, for some very good reason, which you're not prepared to reveal to me." She grabbed his arms as he tried to turn away, forced him to look down into her wide-eyed, furious face. Hazel eyes, widely spaced on either side of the small, strong nose. The eyes that had first attracted him to her as a fellow-student at university, which seemed an age ago now. She was pretty still, despite the years and the children. When he stared into those eyes, and that face that was so alive with the vigour of her anger, he wondered why he had ever needed more than this.

He dropped his head, looked at the small feet in the flat shoes that were so nearly touching his, muttered, "It's difficult, Ros. I'm sorry."

She watched the face that would not look into hers, a boy's face, puzzled because she was denying him, surly because he could not have his own way as usual. A boy's face with the lines of middle age beginning to etch themselves upon it; a contradiction of a face. For a moment, she wanted to mother him, to pull the troubled head down onto her breast, to tell him it would all be all right, that she would do what he wanted. Then she thought of the long days alone with the children, of the nights when he should have been with her and was not, and she said, "You'll need to be a lot more than sorry, Tom, if you want me to help you."

She was more in control of herself than he was, and she felt the power of that. Enjoyed it, indeed. The saint he complained about in her was strangely absent now, and the cruelty she had so often felt in his dismissals was all on her side. She felt almost exultant as she said, "You'll need to tell me where you actually were on that night when you want me to say that we were at the cinema together. Then I'll decide whether you're worth lying for."

Eddie Hurst sat back in his leather swivel chair behind the big desk and smiled. The smile did not reach his eyes, of course. Few of Hurst's smiles did. 'Hurst the Worst' they called him. He knew it, was even proud of it. The soubriquet made him a Titan in the dark worlds he patrolled.

But he felt anything but a champion at the moment, despite the smile he was painting over his alarm. Someone had made a monumental cock-up. He didn't permit those in his association, and heads would roll for this one, in due course. In the meantime, he would have to salvage what he could from the disaster. But he was used to making his own moves in his own time. Now others were calling the shots, and he would have to improvise.

He had to do that so rarely nowadays that he knew it was no longer one of his strengths. He stalled for the time he needed to think. "There must surely be some mistake, gentlemen." He managed to get an edge of contempt on to that word 'gentlemen', but there was no substance to his mockery, and they knew it as well as he did. He eyed the button beneath his desk, within three inches of his left foot. If he pressed that, two of his gorillas would appear within seconds, full of muscular violence, prepared to intimidate, to beat men senseless, to do worse than that, if he commanded them. But they were useless to him in this situation, and he knew it.

Lambert said calmly, "There's no mistake, Hurst. We have a tape of the telephone conversation. Beautifully recorded. It will ring out crystal clear in court. Offering all kinds of sexual services for money. Suggesting that drugs might be available. It's a little gem, in its own way."

"And what makes you think a respectable businessman like me is in any way connected with such enterprises?"

Bert Hook looked up from his notebook. "Surely you can do better than that, Eddy? I'm not even bothering to record that. Why don't you try again?" This man had evaded the law so often, had brought misery into so many lives, that they were enjoying this. In Bert Hook's cricketing terms, Hurst was on the back foot and dodging about. And the wicket was getting worse for him.

150

Lambert smiled at the man who was trying to remain calm, to see a way out of this. "Your front people at Cotswold Rendezvous soon told us who pulled the strings, Eddy. Natural enough, really: they didn't fancy going down for years to save your miserable skin. We just leant a little, and they gave. No retribution from you, by the way: that would get you deeper in the shit than ever. Submerge you, perhaps; a service to society, that would be."

"Cotswold Rendezvous is a perfectly legitimate singles agency. Providing a service which many people—"

"Of course it is." Lambert was suddenly weary of the preliminaries. "As a front, it's perfect. The first contact our man was offered was a perfectly legitimate one, a lonely lady in search of company. Then your staff got a little too enthusiastic. Began offering things that were anything but legal. And succeeded in dropping their boss right in it." He smiled. "You can hear the tape, if you want. Your lawyer can have a copy, in due course."

Hurst found that his brain was working, at last. They knew about the prostitution. About the supply of young girls. About the rent boys. If they didn't have the evidence now, they'd have it within a few hours: he'd heard already about the enquiries being made in Cheltenham and Gloucester. These people talked, when they were squeezed. So did the landlords whose premises he had used for these services. They weren't real villains, any more than the young men and women who were paid to offer their bodies. You couldn't hope to keep the lid on this, now.

But he might still get away with the drugs. They'd said the tape merely "suggested" that drugs were on offer. That empire was much more lucrative, and much easier to defend. They might get a few small-time suppliers, but that wouldn't implicate him: not legally. Most of them didn't even know where the crack and ecstasy they pushed came from. Even he didn't know some of the barons who supplied him from the Continent. It was safer not to know: that was the way this vast, illegal industry operated. These CID men knew about his involvement, had known for years, but had never be able to prove it in court. And they might still not be able to do so, even now, if he played this carefully and then got his well-paid legal bodyguards on to the task. Admit to the prostitution, play it down as supplying a little harmless fun, mistaken maybe, but not too serious. They had a judge and a barrister among their clients, and that might yet prove useful, if the thing came to court with his name still attached to it.

Hurst sighed. "All right. We offer a service. Provide randy men with what they want. Hardly a hanging matter, is it? Keeps them off the streets and prevents them from propositioning innocent citizens, if you ask me."

"We don't. And you've got yourself involved in a murder investigation this time, Hurst, I'm glad to say."

Hurst felt his pulse quicken a little at that word, in spite of his surface calmness. The mention of the oldest and darkest of crimes had an effect, even on people like him. He knew that the number of police personnel employed leapt dramatically as soon as a death became a murder, that they would delve into all kinds of unwelcome corners as they sought the evidence for a conviction. He had had men killed in his time, of course. That was almost a badge of office, an assertion of status in the murky world he inhabited. But always they had been men who wouldn't be missed, small-time villains whose deaths would be shrugged away by a police force who knew they had little chance of establishing the facts of death. And always Eddie Hurst had been able to distance himself so far from these swift eliminations that no one could ever have brought them back to him.

This was different. An implication in a death which was outside his control and influence. He said, "I haven't killed anyone. It's ludicrous that you should suggest it. If—"

"Not directly, perhaps. But if you're implicated, we shall be able to examine all your activities. In detail." Lambert seemed to find that as attractive a prospect as it was a dismal one for the man on the other side of this absurdly large desk.

"I don't know why you should even think—"

"Was a girl called Alison Watts on your books?"

Hurst found himself licking dry lips, a reaction he had always been happy to see in others. Better to sacrifice this, to let the whole of the prostitution and paedophile empire go, if it came to it, than to let them get into the drugs. He was certain of that now. Yet he had to force out the words: it came hard to him to admit anything to the pigs he had laughed at for so long. "I believe she was, yes."

"She was murdered at the end of July. Perhaps you were involved in that, too."

"Of course I wasn't. The first I knew about the girl's death was when I read about it in the press last week."

"But Alison Watts was earning you a lot of money. You must have known months ago that she'd gone missing."

Hurst considered whether he should deny that, whether he should try even at this stage to distance himself from the network of vice, to let someone else take the rap for pimping. But there wasn't anyone else, now. And these men weren't going to take their teeth out until they had tasted blood. He made himself smile. "Our staff leave us for all kinds of reasons, without always informing us about them. They get married, sometimes. Or move to the other end of the country. There is a high turnover rate among nubile young girls. Attractive women with a little money have plenty of options. But perhaps you wouldn't know about that." He managed a token sneer.

"We have search warrants for your offices in Gloucester and Cheltenham. We shall take a list from you of the males and females you employ for improper purposes. In due course, they will all be interviewed. At this moment, I am interested in the murder of Alison Watts. I need a list of the men who were prepared to pay for the services you offer. The kind of men who might have had contact with girls like Alison."

Hurst delayed them a little, for form's sake. He could have made it difficult for them to find the list, could even have destroyed certain documents while they went for their search warrants. In other circumstances, he would certainly have done so. But the destruction of evidence when a superintendent was in pursuit of murder suspects gave pause for thought, even to Eddy Hurst. Especially when the list would at least remove him from any immediate implication in this death. Within five minutes, they had a list of thirty-three names in their hands.

Most of them were names which meant nothing to them, though doubtless most of them were affluent citizens who would be highly embarrassed by the questioning which was to come.

But halfway down the list was a name which immediately caught their eyes. It was that of Thomas Murray, pillar of respectable society and Head Teacher of Oldford Comprehensive School.

153

Chapter Seventeen

CHRISTINE Lambert watched her husband finishing his breakfast as solicitously as she had once watched the daughters who now had children of their own. He hunched a little over the table nowadays, and he no longer complained about the absence of bacon and egg or the presence of semi-skimmed milk. Even as a joke, that ritual had been exhausted. She had got her flowers for his forgetfulness about her cancer clearance. The white and yellow chrysanthemums glistened in the hearth as they caught the pale morning sun. His omission was no more than a joke between them now; she had long since ceased to look for issues of dissent between them.

As she watched him climb stiffly into the old Vauxhall he clung to like a comfortable jacket, she wondered what the future held for them. What on earth would John do, once he had to give up the work which had so dominated his life? He read a lot, when they were on holiday, but holiday habits were notoriously difficult to transfer to retirement. He liked his garden, as she did, but they wouldn't need to spend much more time on it than they did now. He said he'd had his fill of study courses, and he wasn't a great one for the theatre.

He had his golf, of course. That would get him out from under her feet and help to keep both of them sane and civilised. Christine went into the hall and rang Eleanor Hook. "Bert left?" she said cautiously. He had, of course. "How's the golf going?"

Eleanor laughed. "Bert says it's the most stupid game ever invented. But I think he's longing to have another go, really. I found him swinging a club in the back garden and he looked like a schoolboy caught with his hand in the fridge. They're just big kids, aren't they, underneath?"

"And long may it remain so! I'll get John to drag him out again, as soon as they have time with this Alison Watts case. As long as I know that it isn't really purgatory for him."

"Oh, it's purgatory all right. But I think he has an idea he daren't voice that he may win through to heaven in the end. They never learn, do they?"

"Just as well for us that they don't, Eleanor. I've been thinking about the future, when both of them are retired and likely to be sitting at home. We need to make some plans for them."

"God, what a prospect! A few years away yet, God and the Home Secretary willing. But I suppose we need to plan, as the pension adverts tell us."

Christine asked about the Hooks' children, who were only thirteen and twelve. Bert had married late and happily, and Eleanor was eight years younger than him. The two wives made plans to drag their husbands off to see *King Lear* at Stratford early in the new year. That parable of old age going wrong would be a warning to people with the shadow of retirement impinging, Christine Lambert pointed out.

She made her preparations then for her afternoon's teaching. John grumbled that she spent almost as much time on the half-time post as she had when she was working five days a week, but she found that she was getting much more satisfaction and enjoyment from her work, now that she was relaxed.

As she lifted the heavy briefcase on to the table, the side of her chest gave her a swift stab of pain, and she clutched automatically at the lung below the breast which had been removed six months earlier. It was good that John should have plenty to do in his retirement. She might not always be here to program him. You never knew, in this life.

In the garden behind the square 1930s house, Jason Bullimore paced up and down the lawn, pretending to inspect the last flowers of the year on the roses. He was like an anxious father awaiting the birth of his first child, thought his sister as she watched him through the window. She could not see Jason following the modern trend and being present at the birth: too much blood and pain and realism for him in that.

He was still a boy in many things, if you knew him as well as she did.

Barbara Bullimore felt the familiar mixture of affection and frustration as she watched her brother's nervousness through the double glazing. She had needed to be a mother to him ever since they lost their parents, making a mother's allowances and a mother's sacrifices. She would never give up her own career, but she had subordinated it to that of her brilliant younger brother when he came down from Oxford, taking a library post near to his school so that they could set up house together, securing a sideways move to the Gloucestershire Library Service when he had had to move because of that ridiculous business with the girls in Wiltshire. She would have been much further up her own career ladder by now if it hadn't been for supporting Jason like this. But it was what her parents would have wanted, and she was content that it should be so. She just hoped, as she watched him fingering the plants on the trellis, that this latest mess he'd got himself involved in wasn't going to require even more sacrifices from her.

For Jason, it was almost a relief when his anxious ears heard the police car turn into the gravelled drive on the other side of the house. He went swiftly through the kitchen and the hall and opened the front door almost at the moment when Bert Hook rang the bell. "Good morning," said John Lambert. "Or is it now good afternoon? Anyway, we thought it would be better to see you here in your lunch hour than at the school. Fewer prying eyes; fewer wagging tongues."

"Quite. You remember my sister, Barbara?"

"Indeed, yes. But we need to see you alone, Mr Bullimore."

Barabara Bullimore, standing foursquare in the door of the lounge with the light behind her like some formidable automaton, looked for a moment as if she might argue. Then she said, "Of course you do, Superintendent. I shall be in the dining room, in the unlikely event of your requiring me."

Jason took them into the lounge, invited them to sit down, and shut the door carefully behind him. He looked rather more at ease without his formidable sister, but, with his slight figure and his rather epicene good looks, he again seemed much younger than his twenty-nine years. A man perhaps, who made use of his air of naivety, who was reluctant to accept maturity because it might bring with it the responsibility which he found so hard to accept. Many criminals had a personality like that. Some of them panicked and performed violent acts which appeared to surprise themselves as much as everyone around them.

Jason was aware that they were studying his every move. He found it disconcerting. It made him self-conscious in a way that he could not remember in himself since he had been a child. Under this dispassionate scrutiny, every gesture he made felt like an artificial stage move. He found himself throwing his arms too wide, smiling his youthful smile too broadly, as he sat down and said, "What can I do for you, gentlemen?"

Lambert glanced at Hook, who said, "We thought you might want to change the statement you made, in certain important respects."

Jason looked what he hoped was suitably blank. "I can't think that I would want to change anything I told you last time you came here. You seemed already to know more about me than was comfortable for me. I told you everything that was relevant about Alison Watts and me. At least I think I did. I was certainly very frank with you, as I think you would concede."

Lambert said drily, "You appeared to be so, certainly. Only the speaker knows exactly how honest he is being with us, at the time of an interview. We form our own opinions, of course. And we take statements from a lot of people, in the course of a murder investigation. Almost inevitably, we find that some of these contradict each other. And the points of difference are always of compelling interest to us, as you would expect."

Jason nodded, following each phrase of the explanation, almost enjoying it. This meeting of minds reminded him of the long nights in his room at Oxford, where they had argued into the small hours about all kinds of theoretical propositions. Those had been the happiest years of his life. He had to remind himself that this situation was practical, not theoretical, that there might be danger for him in the quiet pronouncements of these intelligent, seemingly friendly men. He tried to resist the impulse to fence intellectually with his opponents. He said, "You're saying that someone else's statement conflicts in some respect with mine? In some important respect, I presume, or you wouldn't be here."

Lambert nodded, smiling slightly. "You have pin-pointed the issue admirably, Mr Bullimore. Would you tell us again when you last saw Alison Watts alive?"

That word "alive" was not lost on Jason. He winced a little, then gave a wry, answering smile, like one acknowledging a debating point well made. "Certainly. It was on Thursday, the twenty-second of July. The day before the end of term. The day before she disappeared."

"That is what we recorded in your original statement. Do you feel any need to change that time now?"

Jason's blue eyes opened a little wider. He looked from one to the other of the two impassive faces opposite him and brushed with his hand at the single soft curl which strayed over the right of his forehead. If his surprise was an act, it was a good one. He said, "No, I don't want to change what I said. The last time I saw Alison was on the Thursday afternoon. There was morning school on the Friday, but I didn't see her then. Plainly someone else has told you otherwise. I can only say that whoever it might be is lying. I imagine the fact that he or she is lying will be of considerable interest to you, as it would be to me."

"Indeed. But sometimes people are merely mistaken, rather than malicious. You would be surprised at the number of discrepancies we find in statements, Mr Bullimore. Or perhaps you wouldn't: I believe teachers are used to pupils taking away widely differing impressions of what they have been told."

It was almost friendly. Certainly it was more relaxed than he had expected. But Jason was curious still to know who had tried to land him deeper in this dangerous swamp. He said, "Someone has obviously told you that I saw Alison later than that Thursday."

"Yes. Later even than the Friday morning. The person involved thinks that Alison saw you on the Friday night. That would make you the last person we know to have seen her alive. If it were true, of course."

The atmosphere in the comfortably furnished room, previously unnaturally relaxed, was suddenly taut. Jason, feeling the silence stretching as they watched him, was drawn into words, almost

158

as if it was his line in the stage drama he still could not quite dismiss from his thoughts. "And where is this – this last meeting supposed to have taken place?"

"That we don't know. If you hadn't arranged to see her, it seems possible that Alison might have come to see you here. Perhaps early on that Friday evening."

Bullimore looked annoyed. Then his too-revealing face lightened, like that of a boy who suddenly sees a winning move at chess. "She wouldn't have found anyone here, even if she came. Barbara was working late, and I wasn't here. What's more, I have a witness. I was having a couple of end-of-term drinks with a colleague, in the White Hart in Oldford. Member of my department, as a matter of fact. Young Fred Souter. He'll confirm it for you, I'm sure." He beamed at them with a relief that was all too evident.

"What time was this, Mr Bullimore?"

"We were there about an hour and a half, I should think. It was meant to be just a quick one, but these things stretch a bit. I should think we were in there from about six-thirty until eight. Fred will tell you."

They could check that with his young colleague, and try to get independent witnesses at the pub, in case he had set this story up with Fred Souter. That would be difficult, though, after all this time. It didn't get him off the hook, by any means, of course. It merely meant he hadn't been with her in that part of the evening. He could have seen her later, might indeed have murdered her and dumped her in the river later on that summer night. Murder often needed darkness to cloak its movements.

"Did you see Alison later in the evening? After you'd left the White Hart?"

"No. I imagine from what I've heard that she'd gone off to the fleshpots of Cheltenham or Gloucester by then. She might have come here and found no one in, of course. Barbara wasn't in until late on that particular Friday."

Lambert, watching the delight of this immature young man as he thought he was outwitting them in an intellectual cat-and-mouse game, was suddenly irritated by him. He said, "You must have

159

noticed that Alison Watts was suddenly rather affluent in the last few months of her life."

Jason was immediately more guarded. "I told you, I didn't see a lot of her in those months. Our affair ended in January."

"You did tell us that, yes. But you also told us that you made attempts to renew the relationship. That you even entertained ideas that you might eventually marry the girl."

"But I didn't actually see much of Alison, except in school. I was aware that she seemed to have some very good clothes – not much more than that."

"And you didn't speculate about the source of her new affluence."

"No. At least – well, I wondered about what she did at weekends, even at the time."

"I see. Well, you were right to wonder, as it turns out, Mr Bullimore. We are now certain that Miss Watts was selling her favours for considerable sums on Friday and Saturday nights. Not walking the streets, like other misguided girls. Her assignations were in comfortable flats. They were set up for her, through an agency run by a man who will no doubt be appearing in court, in due course, on a variety of charges."

It was brutal, but calculated. They watched Bullimore's open face flinch as if it had been struck physically. His small hand brushed angrily at the single curl on his forehead again. He looked for a moment as if he would deny these things on the dead girl's behalf. Then he dropped his hands helplessly to his sides. "It's what I suspected, I suppose. It still comes as a shock. She was so young – so innocent-looking."

He wasn't the first man to say that in that dazed way. And these were the very qualities for which the girl had been recruited by Eddie Hurst, of course. The qualities other, less handsome men than Jason Bullimore were prepared to pay for. He would be less likely to deny what they had to put to him now, whilst he was reeling still from this. Lambert said, "We know that Alison also had other illegal sources of income. Blackmail, if we give it its proper name."

"No. I don't believe that."

"It's true, I'm afraid. We have already identified at least one

160

victim. And we are told that she was planning to blackmail you. To extort money from you by threatening to reveal the details of your affair to others. She was shrewd enough to know that could be harmful to you, could end your teaching career, in view of your previous indiscretions with female pupils. Our informant believes that Alison was planning to see you, to put pressure on you for money, on that last Friday night."

"She didn't. I was in the White Hart."

"You still say she didn't see you after that?"

"No. I've told you. I didn't see her after Thursday morning."

Another pause. another of those long assessments which Jason found so disconcerting. Then Lambert said, "Have you any idea who killed Alison Watts?"

"No. Perhaps the person who told you these lies about me. Whoever that was."

They left him then, seeing themselves out because he was too shaken to accompany them. They half-expected his sister to appear to usher them off the premises, but she was nowhere to be seen.

Barbara Bullimore came and stood beside her trembling brother as they watched the police car drive away. He did not look at her as he said brokenly, "They wanted to know if I'd seen Alison on that last night. They said she was trying to – to get money from me—"

"To blackmail you. Yes, I heard. Heard it all." She glanced towards the serving hatch which connected the two rooms, on the other side of which she had listened with mounting, helpless horror. "Oh, Jason, what a fool you are! To have ever got yourself involved with a slut like that. Even to be thinking of marrying her, apparently. What on earth are you going to do with yourself, if ever I'm not here to protect you?"

161

Chapter Eighteen

DI RUSHTON was happy. He was back at his computer, feeding in the bewildering variety of information which continued to accumulate around the murder of Alison Watts, working out his own system of cross-referencing the different items to search for significant correlations.

That awful evening with Sharon was now no more than a memory: a memory which would not easily fade, it is true, but with no long-term repercussions for him. Indeed, it seemed that something positive had come out of it, after all, thanks to the over-enthusiastic follow-up by that woman who had been rash enough to try to sell him sexual services over the telephone. In a year's time, he might even be able to speak of himself as the undercover man who had initiated the coup which had put Eddie Hurst behind bars at last. He might even have that magic word 'Versatility' on his file when the Promotions Board came to consider his potential to act as a Chief Inspector.

Today, he was even happy to see Superintendent Lambert and Sergeant Hook, who had so enjoyed his unease in the role they had devised for him at Cotswold Rendezvous. For he had things to report to the chief. "Still more money for Alison Watts," he said cheerfully. "She had not one but two building society accounts, as well as the account she opened at Barclays. As we already know, there is over two thousand pounds in the Cheltenham and Gloucester Building Society account, most of it deposited in the six months before her death."

Lambert looked at the details on the print-out. "That will be from her weekend activities in the Eddie Hurst set-up. The C and G is an appropriate institution for her to patronise, in view of the towns where she accumulated her wealth!"

"We've now turned up a new account with the Halifax. There's another thousand in that. Most of it accumulated over the last year. Would that be from her blackmailing activities?"

"Could be. A girl with a tidy mind, our Alison was. She's quite likely to have kept separate accounts for her different entrepreneurial activities."

"There's very little in the Barclays account. And not too many transactions."

"That will be the one she kept for public perusal. That's why we found it in her room. No suspicion aroused there, if her mother should happen to come across it at home," said Hook.

"The question is, where are the books for these building society accounts," said Lambert. "They weren't at her home."

"Removed by Robert Watts?" suggested Rushton.

"Possible, but unlikely. If he'd had those books, I'm sure he'd have been tempted to try to get at the money by now. I should think it's someone who merely wished to conceal the evidence of Alison Watt's money-making activities. Whilst she was merely a missing person, that was successful: it's only when this became a murder investigation that the details have come out."

Rushton said stubbornly, "It could still be Robert Watts. He'd have no wish for his wife to discover that his stepdaughter had been extracting money from him, and start asking why."

"Certainly it's possible. I just think it's unlikely that a man like Watts would have resisted trying to get money out of those accounts, as the months passed. And there are other candidates. Jamie Allen had no wish to see the girl he treasured exposed as a whore. Neither, in a rather different way, had Jason Bullimore, if we're to believe his story that he still entertained rather vague and romantic notions that he might marry the wench. And what about her headmaster at the school, Thomas Murray, who took away the contents of Alison's locker and was paying Eddie Hurst for sexual services supplied? The sooner we see that naughty lad the better."

Rushton brightened. "We've got some details now of Murray's involvement. They called this offshoot of Cotswold Rendezvous 'Gold Star Services'. Murray seems to have used it to meet young girls for what they called 'Straight sex of all kinds' at intervals of about six weeks."

"I don't suppose he could afford it much more often, with the prices being asked for 'Quality and Discretion'."

"Any evidence of meetings with Alison Watts?"

"No. Discretion being one of the other watchwords of the organisation, it's possible that neither of them knew that the other was involved."

"Or that Alison found out about her respected headmaster and saw an ideal opportunity to add to her blackmail list."

"Alison worked regularly for Gold Star Services, on almost every Friday night and many Saturdays. No wonder she was making money so fast."

"But not quite as fast as Hurst the Worst, no doubt," said Lambert grimly. "When was her last appointment?"

"On the night of Friday the twenty-third of July. She should have received a visitor in her regular plush love-nest in Cheltenham at nine o'clock on that night. She never turned up. Gold Star had to smooth down a disgruntled and frustrated customer. A consultant psychiatrist, as a matter of fact."

"And they say that sex is all in the mind! It looks more and more likely that Alison Watts was either dead by then, or died within an hour or so afterwards. But we shall only be able to prove that when we find her killer."

Rushton liked that. Not if, but when. He and John Lambert might temperamentally be miles apart, but they both relished the hunt. Chris knew how far his career had progressed in the team of this man whom he sometimes found so irritating. He said, "Jamie Allen is still the last person we know to have seen Alison Watts alive. At about six-thirty, according to his account."

"And they had what he admits was a blazing row. What about Jamie's claim that she was going off to see Jason Bullimore, with a view to blackmail?"

"We've checked Bullimore's story that he was in the White Hart at the time in question. His colleague, Fred Souter, confirms that the two of them were drinking together early on that Friday night. Reviewing arrangements for the following year's teaching before they each went off on holiday, it seems. He can't be absolutely

164

sure of the time, but he thinks about six-thirty until eight or a little later. It's still possible that Bullimore saw Alison after they'd left the pub, of course."

"Possible, certainly. For all we know, they had a meeting arranged. But if she was intending to be in Cheltenham at nine, ready for action with a randy psychiatrist, it seems unlikely."

Rushton, who hated uncertainties, said reluctantly, "She could have been killed in Cheltenham, of course. Or anywhere between Oldford and Cheltenham. We don't know what happened to her after six-thirty."

"I wonder where the girl's headmaster was on that night," said Lambert. "My guess is that he was in Cheltenham himself on the evening of the twenty-third, though he hasn't admitted it. If he was, it would put him right in the frame. We shall see what he has to say about that, in a little while."

Rushton said, "Robert Watts has still no alibi for that night. He says vaguely that he was probably drinking, but, unlike Jason Bullimore, he has produced no witness to the fact."

Lambert levered himself rather stiffly upright and looked at his watch. "It's time for our next meeting with the ungracious Mr Watts," he said.

Number One, The Lawns looked rather more cared for than on their previous visits. The grass at the front of the square house had been cut, the edges trimmed back to a semblance of straightness. Hook had arranged the time for this meeting, and Robert Watts must have been waiting anxiously for their arrival. The door of the blank box of a house opened to them well before they had time to ring the bell, and the householder stood nervously on the step. He was in shirt sleeves, despite the sharpness of the day, but the cuffs of his thick cotton tartan shirt were buttoned and his greying hair was neatly combed, even slicked flat over his temples with water.

His old belligerence to the police was still there, but it was little more than a ritual defiance now. "You'd best come through, I suppose," he said, in his surly fashion.

He led them into the square lounge, where there were changes apparent from the occasion two days previously when they had last confronted him here. There were no empty beer cans. The floor was newly vacuumed. The film of dust which had sheened the television set and the polished wood of the mantelpiece was gone, and there was a vase of spray carnations in the empty hearth.

But the most significant change of all was a human one. Kate Watts sat in the chair nearest to the window, looking up at them apprehensively as they entered the room, like a child who expected to be chastised for her weakness in returning here. She wore a rather showy paisley dress, not at all the type of garment one wore for housework, and they knew immediately that she had dressed up for their visit. The damage to her face was almost repaired. The swelling on her nose had subsided, the bruising had disappeared, and the make-up was skilfully enough applied for the healing cuts to be almost invisible now on her watchful face. Any casual observer would scarcely have detected that this woman had been hit so hard so recently.

Lambert nodded to her. "Good afternoon, Mrs Watts. Nice to see you looking better." He would make no comment on the wisdom or otherwise of her return to this house. It was not his business, and as always when he neared the climax of a murder investigation, he was becoming more blinkered in the pursuit of his quarry.

He turned to her husband. "We are much nearer to finding out who killed Alison now," he said calmly. "The evening of Friday the twenty-third of July is the crucial time, as I indicated it might be when we spoke to you last. We have still not been able to establish any clear account of your movements on that night. You said last time we were here that you weren't even sure of them yourself. I now ask you again to tell us where you were and at what times on that night."

Kate Watts looked at him anxiously, even fearfully, as if the formality of Lambert's challenge alarmed her. Was it possible that she had never considered until now that her husband might be asked to give an account of himself as a suspect in Alison's death? He did not return her glance but said stubbornly, "I don't know. It's too long ago. I didn't kill her, you know. And I told you everything I could last time." Only then did he glance sideways at

166

his wife. "Look, there's no need for Kate to be involved in this, is there? She's been upset quite enough already."

In his clumsy way, he was trying to protect her, thought Lambert. So Kate Watts hadn't discussed his abuse of her daughter with him yet; probably he still thought she didn't know about it. And if they hadn't spoken of the abuse, Kate wouldn't know about the money Alison had extracted from her husband. He wondered if this fragile relationship could possibly survive the revelations which must surely fall upon it soon. Before he could say anything, Kate said, surprisingly calmly, "I want to stay, Superintendent Lambert. I want to know all about my daughter, you see. And most of all, I want to know who killed her." She glanced at her husband, did not return his small, nervous smile. Hook wondered if she suspected Robert Watts of dispatching Alison from the world, if she had returned home to be present when he was arrested.

Lambert looked at her for a moment, trying to estimate her emotional stability. Then he gave the briefest of nods and said to her husband, "If you can't tell us where you were on that night, we need to check with you on your last contact with Alison, to see if you have any better idea than others we have talked to of her movements on that night."

He said sullenly, 'I've told you all I have to say. I don't see—"

"I can tell you about the last time Alison was here, about what she was doing then," said Kate Watts unexpectedly. "No one has troubled to ask me much about it. Perhaps they thought I would be too upset to give them anything useful."

Hook, preparing to write, thought that she had the calm which descends upon people when they summon concentration during moments of extreme stress. Probably when all this was over, when they had gone, she would collapse into weeping; he wondered whether Robert Watts would be able to provide her with any consolation or would be angrily thrust aside.

Kate Watts said, "Alison was here until about half past five, quarter to six perhaps. She was getting her clothes ready to go off into Cheltenham. I was worried about that, but as usual she wouldn't tell me who she was meeting. Then that boy came round.

The one from the school. She'd finished with him, I thought, but he kept hanging around."

"Jamie Allen?"

"That's him. Well, he came round and persuaded her to go out for a walk with him. I don't think she wanted to go, but perhaps she thought she might finally get rid of him, if they had it out."

"Did she come back here after that?"

"Yes. At about half past six, I think. But the boy wasn't with her. She said she'd sent him packing, that she didn't expect to see him again. She was quite upset about things he'd said to her, I think."

And perhaps Jamie Allen was even more upset by the things Alison Watts had said to him, Lambert thought grimly. "And when did she go out again, Mrs Watts?"

Kate Watts pursed her lips, glanced at her husband, looked back at Hook's ball-pen poised over his notebook, as if she knew the importance of this and was determined to get it right. She was surprisingly calm, for a mother who must at least suspect by now that she was talking about her daughter's last hours on earth, but no doubt she had reviewed these events in her own mind many times over the weeks since her daughter had disappeared from her life. "She wasn't in the house very long. I remember she grumbled a bit about Jamie and the way he'd thrown her schedule out. She said she'd probably have to get a taxi – I remember that because I told her she shouldn't be so extravagant."

"And what was her reaction?"

"She just laughed at me. You know, the way girls do. Said I should get used to thinking big, that she didn't intend to be poor like us for the rest of her life." She glanced across at Robert Watts again, as if she feared he might take this as a slur on his ability as a breadwinner, but he kept his eyes unblinkingly on the carpet in front of his feet. Plainly Kate knew nothing of the money her daughter had wrested from Robert Watts.

"Did she call a taxi?"

"Not from here, she didn't. She showered and changed and rushed out of the house again. She couldn't have been here much more than twenty minutes."

"So she left here at what time?"

"About ten to seven, I suppose."

They would check the local taxi firms again, of course, though they had already drawn a blank there. Drivers would remember a pretty girl in the early evening normally, but it was the old problem of scents gone cold. Few people had clear recall after an interval as long as eleven weeks. But perhaps this time they would be able to suggest a few possible destinations to jog the memory of the drivers.

"Do you know where she planned to go to in this taxi, Mrs Watts?"

"No. She was getting more and more secretive about the places she went to. Especially at the weekends." For the first time, tears brimmed in her eyes. "I wish I'd pressed her harder about that, now. She might still have been alive today, if I'd been able to control where she went."

It was a sentiment both the CID men had heard before, in similarly tragic circumstances. They made soothing noises, said that they didn't think anything Kate Watts might have done would have prevented this particular death. Eventually she collected herself, wiped her eyes, nodded two or three times, as if trying to convince herself of that, and said, "I don't know that she got a taxi at all, you know. She might have said she was going to get one just to annoy me."

And even if she had taken a taxi, she could have used it to take her back to Jamie Allen as easily as to take her to the house where she expected to find Jason Bullimore; she could have gone to see this increasingly dubious headmmaster of hers, Thomas Murray; she might even have journeyed to meet her stepfather, Robert Watts, who was still unable or unwilling to provide any account of his own whereabouts on that night.

Watts stayed sitting upon the settee in the lounge, unwilling to meet their eyes, as Kate Watts showed them out. She shut the lounge door behind them, whispered in the hall, "I've come back to him, as you can see. They all advised against it, but I think we'll be all right, now that he's had a shock." Her hand strayed automatically to the bruises that had almost disappeared now from her face and she glanced swiftly at the oblong mirror

169

in the hall as they passed it. "He's a good man, really, you know – just a bit weak when things get on top of him. He says he loves me, and I believe him."

They didn't argue with her: they knew the statistics about battered wives, but they weren't social workers. They couldn't tell her how to come to terms with a stepfather's abuse, still less about how to deal with her daughter's extortion of money from him. And how would the knowledge that her darling Alison had worked as a high-class prostitute for one of the area's most notorious villains affect the fragile health of Kate Watts? It was a relief that their first, indeed their only, concern must be whether the limited and now tortured Robert Watts had killed his stepdaughter.

Kate Watts thanked them for their efforts, smiled a farewell to them from her doorstep. Then she turned back into the house and the still unsuspected horrors which lay ahead of her.

Chapter Nineteen

A check of the Oldford taxi firms revealed nothing. No one remembered Alison Watts. If, as Kate Watts had suggested, her daughter had taken to regular use of taxis, someone should have remembered a pretty girl like Alison, even if they could not recall the particular occasion of Friday, 23 July. No one did. Wearily, DI Rushton began a second trawl through the much longer list of hire car firms in Cheltenham and Gloucester.

In due course this would mean a second, probably fruitless, series of enquiries for the officers on the edge of the case, who were probably losing interest as they began to feel themselves peripheral to an investigation which had centred increasingly upon the school and the home of the dead girl, despite the luridness now revealed in her weekend activities.

The four men who had been repeatedly questioned knew now that they were suspects, and they watched, waited and wondered. They wondered about the extent of police knowledge, about what moves were going on without their knowledge to press the enquiry forward. Robert Watts struggled with the thought of what he had done with Alison and the police knowledge that he had paid her to keep quiet about it. With his battered wife newly returned home, it was not the best basis for a new beginning. Jason Bullimore and Jamie Allen, fulfilling their different functions in the daily life of Oldford Comprehensive School, moved like men treading an unreal world. Alison's death and the thrusting progress of the investigation lay over everything for them, reducing what might have seemed important in staffroom and classroom to a charade, played out whilst they waited for the next and final instalment in the real-life drama which had caught them up.

And Superintendent Lambert and Detective Sergeant Hook,

171

hustling forward the action of this drama, drove out to see the wife of the fourth man, the Headmaster of Oldford Comprehensive School.

She was waiting anxiously for their arrival. They saw her pale, pretty face at the window of the room to the right of the porch as they went up the path to the front door. A nice sheltered spot this, the gardener in Hook noted automatically. Even this late in the season, the rich red Gloucestershire soil was still thrusting its nourishment into the roses which bloomed prolifically around the porch of Cotswold stone.

She stood in the doorway before they reached it, taut with stress, forcing a small, mirthless smile, in a parody of a normal social greeting. "Ros Murray," she said, before they reached her. Then, because she did not know how to behave at a meeting like this, she thrust out her hand stiffly towards them. Each of them shook it in turn as Lambert introduced them. Hook said, "It was good of you to see us at such short notice, Mrs Murray."

She said, "I preferred that we should have this meeting while the children were out at school." Not to mention their father, they thought. She offered them tea, because again she did not know what was expected of her in these strange circumstances.

Lambert smiled and refused. "This needn't take long," he said.

Ros sat on the edge of her chair, smoothing down the creases of her trousers over her knees, conscious of her hands as she couldn't recall ever being conscious of them before. They were not part of her; they were things on the end of her arms which seemed to have a life of their own, which seemed to be intent on betraying her by waving ridiculously in the air without any command from her brain. She folded her arms determinedly, then found that her hands were back on her knees unbidden within seconds. These men did not seem unfriendly. But they watched her, unashamedly, and she became conscious of her every movement.

It was the one with the rounded, rubicund features, the one who did not seem threatening at all, who said to her, "We are here because we should like to establish what your husband was doing on the night of Friday, July the twenty-third. I know it's quite a long time ago, but if you could—"

172

"More than eleven weeks ago. Not many people could remember what they were doing on a particular night, at this distance in time."

"No. That is quite true. But we understood that—"

"And lots of people couldn't provide you with alibis, you know. It doesn't mean that they're not perfectly innocent."

Lambert intervened. "That's true, of course it is. We find it demonstrated all the time. It's just that when people can show us that they were in a particular place at a certain time, we can eliminate them from some of our enquiries. And we understood that there was a chance that your husband—"

"Tom. Tom was at the cinema with me on that night." She seemed to find no contradiction in this with what she had said earlier. Instead, she went on quickly, almost eagerly, "We went to the multiplex in Gloucester. To see *The English Patient*. Very enjoyable, it was. Not quite as good as I'd expected, though. But other people had been too enthusiastic about it to me, I think."

She trotted the statements out without inflection, like a bad actress reading from a text she had only just seen. Now she paused, as if that text said that there should be a question at this point. Lambert behaved as though he had not read it, and Ros Murray's soft brown eyes switched swift as a bird's from one face to the other of the men before her and back again. There was a long interval before Hook said, "What time would this be, Mrs Murray?"

Ros thought the cue had come at last, even if belatedly and from the wrong person. "We left here at about six-thirty. Had a drink before we went into the cinema, you see. When the film was over, we came straight back here afterwards. We reached here at about eleven. Neither of us went out again." She had rehearsed it carefully, but it would have come out more convincingly if they'd drawn it from her by questions, instead of receiving it in a continuous monologue like this. Still, she got the facts out, as she and Tom had agreed them, and she didn't think she had missed anything vital out. It was a relief to get it over with; she'd told Tom she was no good at this, and she knew now that she was right. Without the little bit of Dutch courage she had administered when she knew the CID men were coming, she wouldn't have managed it at all.

There should have been some reaction from these men, some nods of assent, some acknowledgement that what she had told them was helpful to them. Even some subsidiary questions, maybe even a little doubt that she could assuage, would have been better than this long, assessing silence. When she could stand it no longer, she said, "I can tell you things about the film, if you like. To prove we saw it, I mean. Ask me about anything you like in it."

Lambert sighed. "I'm sure you could tell us all kinds of things about *The English Patient*, Mrs Murray. The important thing for us is whether you saw it on the night of the twenty-third of July."

"We did. I told you we did. Told you the times." The hazel eyes which had stared steadily ahead of her through her recital of the facts were now cast down. Her wide mouth was set in a thin line.

Lambert wondered why worthy women were so often drawn into lies for worthless men, why that particular strand of the human tragedy seemed to be paraded so often before him. He said wearily, "We shall need the name of your baby-sitter, of course."

"Our baby-sitter?"

"Mrs Murray, you have two young children. I'm sure you are far too responsible a mother to have left them unattended for four and a half hours. The person who was with them on that night will be able to confirm your story to us."

Suddenly, she was furious with Tom. He had put her through all this, and yet not even thought of this obvious thing. Or had he asked the girl down the road who sometimes sat for them to lie for him, too? How far did this web of deceit stretch? How many innocent people were to be called upon to lie to protect her husband's precious skin? Ros said dully, "There was no one here that night. Except me. We did go to see *The English Patient* in Gloucester, but not on that night."

Lambert said softly, "No, I thought not. And where was your husband on the night of the twenty-third of July, Mrs Murray?"

The hands which had so troubled Ros lifted from her knees, waved without meeting each other through the air, and fell heavily

174

back on to her thighs. "You'd better ask him about that." She looked up appealingly, fastened upon Hook's large, sympathetic face, which swam a little through the moisture that had sprung to her eyes. "And tell him – oh it doesn't matter! I was going to say tell him that I did my best for him, but what's the use of that?"

She watched them go from the step where she had greeted them, her face a strange mixture of distress and relief. As Lambert marched quickly away down the path, Bert Hook said softly to her, "Next time you feel you need a drink to face people, you'd be better to go for the vodka than the whisky, m'dear. You can't smell vodka on the breath, you see." He gave her a quick smile of sympathy before he followed his rapidly disappearing chief.

They both knew as they drove away that it would be better to get the story of where he had been on that night from Murray himself. For it might be that the truth was even worse than whatever he had confessed it to be to his distraught wife.

Police procedures are neither as rigid nor as effective as Chief Constables and Home Secretaries like to emphasise they are to an anxious public. The machinery and the methods are subject to human error, and they can go horribly wrong, not just in high-profile instances such as that of the Yorkshire Ripper, Peter Sutcliffe, but in less publicised cases as well.

More often than policemen would like to admit, a piece of luck or a piece of stupidity by a criminal – often they are the same thing for the CID – hasten a solution. One such incident now accelerated an arrest in the Alison Watts murder case.

The man looked as if he was already regretting his action when the young WPC ushered him briskly past the murder room and into the office of Detective Inspector Rushton. He wore a leather jacket with the top two buttons undone and fashionably shabby jeans. He had a young man's shambling gait, as if he had not yet cast off the uncoordinated movements which stem from rapid teenage growth; it was the kind of stooping walk which still makes ageing brass-hats scream for national service and army discipline.

Chris Rushton's experienced eye took in a different picture. Not violent, he thought – certainly far too embarrassed to be aggressive here. Not on drugs, for he was clear-eyed and conscious of everything around him. Scruffy, but basically clean, with straight hair which was long enough to drop down over the left side of his face. Vulnerable probably, if you got to him whilst he was still apprehensive. "You've come here to tell us something. Best spit it out, then!" Rushton said briskly. Only then did he indicate that the young man should sit in the chair on the other side of his desk.

"It's – well, it's about this murder case. The Alison Watts one."

"Clearly. You wouldn't have been shown in here if it hadn't been."

"No. Well, it's a bit difficult for me, you see. I'm not quite sure I should be here at all, really. It's – well, it's just from a sense of public duty." He smiled an awful, sickly smile to go with this declaration of civic conscience, then wiped it rapidly away as he saw how fiercely Rushton was glaring at him. "I – I used to give her lifts, you see, Alison. And I heard you were asking round about who might have done that." If he had had a cap, he would no doubt have twisted it between his fingers; as it was, he had to make do with a vigorous wringing of the hands themselves.

Chris Rushton pushed himself back in his chair, trying not to reveal the hope which was surging within him to this callow young sprig. "You mean you've been running an unofficial taxi service. Unregistered. Unlicensed. Plying for hire while not on any official list. Naughty, that."

It was common enough. Men got themselves a roomy car and 'moonlighted', usually at nights when there was plenty of business about for hire cars, often combining the activity with a day job or omitting to declare such earnings when they registered as unemployed. A busy police force generally ignored the practice, unless it was blatant or the registered cabbies insisted upon some action against the cowboy operators. Rushton's fingers ran rapidly over the computer keyboard, opening up a new file. "Better have your name, hadn't we?"

For a moment the man looked as though he would argue. Then he shrugged hopelessly and said "Wayne Hopkins. I was intending—"

"And you say you picked up Alison Watts. When?"

"Well, regularly, I suppose. Friday nights, mostly. And some Saturdays; most Saturdays, I think, over the last few months before she disappeared. And once or twice on Sundays."

"Quite the regular chauffeur for the young lady. Unofficial and unlicensed. And where did you pick up and drop her?"

"I collected her in Cheltenham. At half past eleven at night: always at the same time and from the same place." He gave the name of the apartment, which Rushton didn't trouble to record. It was the same address he had noted elsewhere as the flat where Alison Watts had operated so lucratively for herself and Eddie Hurst. "And where did you take her?"

"Home, always. Well, not quite to the door of her house, but virtually there. I only live round the corner, about a hundred yards from her house. She always got out outside my garage and walked the last bit. She once said she needed a bit of clean air before she faced her mother."

"Do you know what she was doing in Cheltenham?"

The young man reddened. Like his shambling walk earlier, it made him look younger than he was. He was probably about twenty-three, but his embarrassment seemed to take six years off him. "No. I asked her once, but she told me that was her business, not mine."

"It doesn't matter." Alison's activities on those weekends would be public knowledge soon enough now. Rushton kept his voice studiously even as he said, "Did you pick her up from the usual place in Cheltenham at eleven-thirty on that last Friday night, Wayne?"

"No. I should have done, but she wasn't there. I was there on time at half past eleven, but she didn't come down when I rang the bell. And there weren't any lights on in the flat."

Lambert marched impatiently into the now familiar Head Teacher's office at Oldford Comprehensive School. The door was scarcely shut before he said, "You lied to us, Mr Murray. And you asked your wife to lie on your account, making her an accessory."

"She rang me, Superintendent. I'm grateful to you for coming here so quickly, so that we can sort out this misunderstanding."

177

"No misunderstanding, Mr Murray. Deliberate deceit. Obstructing the police in the performance of their duties. Not a good example to set, for a man in your position."

Murray winced automatically at the mention of the public persona he had spent so much of his time polishing over the last ten years. "There is surely no need to take such a high-handed attitude over a little economy with the truth. It was venal of me, even silly of me, I admit, but scarcely more than that." He spread his hands wide, attempting the urbanity he had ceased to feel with the first high-pitched words of his wife's excited phone call to him a quarter of an hour earlier.

"Not so much economical with the truth as contemptuous of it. You lied about your whereabouts at a time when a girl you knew was being murdered. You were not at the multiplex in Gloucester nor at any other cinema on the night of July the twenty-third last. And you were certainly not with your wife."

Murray's blue eyes widened as he stared at his inquisitor. Then, suddenly, his head was in his hands. Whether it was a genuine breakdown in control or whether this despair was assumed to gain a little time for thought was not clear. The CID men were in no mood to waste time puzzling about that. Hook said, "If it helps you to tell the truth, you might as well know that we know all about your involvement with Gold Star Services in Cheltenham."

He looked up at them with that, his blue eyes dry but wild. "You know about that? I – I can't even tell you who ran it, you know, I—"

"We know all about it, Mr Murray," Lambert interrupted. "It's a part of a large criminal empire, run by a man named Eddie Hurst. There will be a court case, in due course. You may very well be one of the prosecution witnesses in it. Unless of course you are then awaiting trial on a charge of murder."

"I didn't kill Alison Watts."

"That has yet to be established. Where were you on the night of the twenty-third of July?"

"In Cheltenham"

"Taking advantage of the pleasures offered by Gold Star Services."

"Yes. Look, Superintendent. I like the company of young women. All right, I like having sex with them. I have a high sex drive, and a job which offers me few opportunities to release it. You must have come across plenty of people like me."

"You also have a loyal wife. More loyal than you deserve, perhaps. But that's not our concern. What interests us is that you removed evidence in the course of a murder investigation. It was you who took away the contents of Alison Watts' locker at school. You who carefully removed the secret things, which she kept at school because she didn't want them discovered at home."

"The building society books, you mean. I didn't destroy them. I have them here under lock and key." He turned the lock in the top drawer of his desk and produced two newish-looking account books for the Halifax and the Cheltenham and Gloucester Building Societies.

Lambert did not take them from him and he put them down on the surface of his desk. They lay like an accusation between the cornered man and his questioners. "Why did you choose to withhold this evidence, Mr Murray?"

"I met Alison in Cheltenham one night, about three months before she disappeared. I knew from where I saw her that she was operating for Gold Star Services. She was going into a flat I'd used myself on a previous occasion for one of my – my assignations. I think she realised a little while later that I was one of the Gold Services clients. She made a remark when I met her in a school corridor that we might eventually meet professionally, in a different context."

"So her disappearance was highly convenient for you. And her death was even more so."

He nodded miserably. "I suppose so. I didn't kill her." His eyes were fixed upon those innocent-looking deposit books at the other side of his desk, as if they might spring up and claw him at any moment.

"Had Alison Watts attempted to blackmail you with the knowledge she had acquired about your sexual excursions?"

He looked up then, wanting to deny it, knowing the admission would take him further into the morass. Then he nodded dully,

"She had a hundred pounds from me, a week before she died. She put it straight in there, I think." He indicated the Halifax book. He shrugged wearily. "I didn't intend any dishonesty when I hid these books. I just thought that if I could hide what she had been up to at the weekends, my own involvement with Gold Star Services might remain secret as well. Alison Watts was only a missing person, not a murder victim, when I hid them, you know."

"Yes. Except that one person at least knew that she was dead. The person who tightened a ligature of some kind around her neck until she could no longer trouble anyone. Were you that person, Mr Murray?"

"No. I may be a lecher, but I'm not a murderer."

He looked at them desperately for some sign of acceptance of that claim. They did not comment. Hook put the bank books into a plastic folder and they left. When the headmaster's secretary took him in his afternoon cup of tea ten minutes later, she thought that Thomas Murray, whom she was used to seeing so breezy and confident, looked like a man at war with himself.

Christopher Rushton was taking great care to get everything he could out of Wayne Hopkins. Someone should have unearthed this shambling young man earlier, but he could dish out the ritual bollockings later. Not only did it look as if the man was pure gold, but he had presented himself personally to Detective Inspector Rushton. It was just as they said, you made your own luck in this game. If you worked hard and systematically, instead of racing round town and countryside like old John Lambert, you collected the occasional piece of good fortune, and deserved it.

He said, "So Alison wasn't there when you went to collect her in Cheltenham at eleven-thirty on that last night. But you ferried her about at other times as well, you say, Wayne?"

"Yes. She used me more and more, over those last few weeks before she disappeared. And she paid me well: almost as much as an official taxi would have cost her. She said she could afford it. Time was money to her, she said. She laughed about that."

"Yes, she would do, I expect. And when was the last time you saw Alison?"

"That's why I'm here. I heard you were asking around about who picked her up on that last Friday, when she disappeared. It was me."

Rushton suppressed a sudden urge to hug this shambles of a man who had appeared so tardily with what might be priceless information. Instead, he looked at him sternly and said, "It's taken you a hell of a long time to remember this. Why didn't you come forward when the girl first went missing?"

The head with its lank hair wobbled unsteadily from side to side. Wayne Hopkins was wondering even now what would happen to him at the end of this. Was it a criminal charge, operating a taxi service without a licence? Even murder becomes secondary to one's own survival, when seen from the perspective of an inexperienced young male who suddenly realises he has not behaved as cleverly as he thought. "Well, she was only a missing person then, wasn't she? I didn't think it was important. And I – well, I thought I might have to give up all the money I'd made by carrying passengers without a licence. I couldn't have done that, you see, 'cause I'd spent it. Bought a newer car." For a moment, his eyes brightened even now with the vision of that sleek maroon Granada which Alison Watts had done so much to provide for him.

Rushton's natural inclination was to keep the lad hopping about. Apprehensive witnesses revealed most, in his book. But he was too eager for information now to worry much about tactics. "So you had Alison Watts in your car on Friday the twenty-third of July last. At what time?"

"She came round to my house and asked for a lift. About quarter to seven. Perhaps just after that, but not much. She said she was running late and needed me to get her back on schedule."

"And where did she ask you to take her, Wayne?"

"An address out on the Hereford road. I dropped her off at the end of a little cul-de-sac just beyond Fownhope. I saw her walking down to the end whilst I was turning the car round. I think she went into the last house. I'd never taken her out there before. I can't tell you whose house it was."

But you don't need to, DI Rushton thought with satisfaction. It was the house of Jason Bullimore.

Chapter Twenty

IT was late afternoon now on this perfect October day. The blue of the sky was deepening; there was not much light left. The air was very still, and there would be a frost before morning. The last of the sun slanted in between the Black Mountains of Wales on his left, dazzling but intermittent, as Lambert drove the old Vauxhall cautiously towards Hereford. There was no hurry now to play out the last scene of this tragic drama. No one else was in danger from this murderer.

When it came into view behind the high cypress hedge, the house of Jason and Barbara Bullimore was as quiet and still as the dying day. There was no sign of movement as the CID officers walked to the front door beside the rectangle of closely mown lawn. The borders had already been cleared of summer bedding at the time of their last visit; now someone had planted wallflowers in neat rows. Too neat, to Hook's mind; they looked in their precisely spaced ranks like soldiers parading in the weedless soil.

There was no sign of any presence in the square 1930s house, no car on the drive in front of the garage. When they rang the bell, the noise rang loud behind the door in what seemed an empty house, and there was no sound of the muffled movements which a ring or a summons often provoked in residents busy about their business. Yet within five seconds of their ringing the bell, the oak door opened, almost noiselessly, and Barbara Bullimore stood imposingly upon the step above them.

"My brother isn't here," she said coldly.

"Maybe it's better that way," said Lambert. He marched unbidden into the house, through into the lounge, with its heavy three-piece suite, its tall pillars of hi-fi speakers, its pictures of the dreaming spires of Oxford. The patio doors were shut now upon the secluded garden, where well-staked dahlias provided brilliant flashes of colour in the twilight, lamps which would be extinguished by the frost which would come with the darkness.

Barbara Bullimore had followed rather than led them into the room. She said, "I suppose you'd better sit down," as ungraciously as she could. But petty rudeness was not her style, and she was clearly disconcerted. When she saw the two tall men seated on the settee, she sat down herself, almost as an afterthought, on the single upright chair in the room. She said with an attempt at contempt, "Well, what progress have you made with your enquiries into the death of this wretched girl?"

It was a mistake. It was not like her to fill silences, and it showed her nervousness, rather than her disdain for these men and the law they represented. Moreover, it emerged as a real enquiry, not the slight on their labours which she had intended. She was genuinely anxious to know how far they had got in their efforts to find the killer of Alison Watts.

Lambert watched her steadily as he said, "We know a lot now about the last movements of Alison Watts on the night she was murdered. We have a picture that is almost complete."

She nodded, looking past them and out of the window, watching a thrush trilling its last song before the night on the top of the lilac tree at the end of the garden. "Really. And what brings you here to disturb my day off from the rigours of the library service?"

"Alison hired a car to bring her to this house on the last evening of her life."

"Really? You surprise me, Superintendent. At what time is this visit supposed to have taken place?"

"Alison arrived here at about seven o'clock."

Barbara Bullimore's broad face allowed itself a smile, not of triumph, but certainly of satisfaction. "Then she was out of luck, Mr Lambert. I worked late on that Friday, and my brother wasn't here either at that time. I believe he was having a drink with one of his colleagues. But I think you already know that: he told me yesterday that you had been asking him about it."

"We did indeed. And we have since had confirmation of his movements from the colleague he was with on that evening."

"Then forgive me, Superintendent, but I don't see that we can be of any further help to you. If the girl did indeed come here, she obviously found no one at home and went on elsewhere."

"No, Miss Bullimore."

"But yes, Mr Lambert. I tell you my brother—"

"I told you that we checked on Jason's whereabouts on that night. We also checked on yours. You weren't working."

She folded her arms, stiffened her back until it was even straighter. "That doesn't mean I was here."

Lambert looked at her evenly. "You were here, weren't you? Alison Watts was last seen coming into this house. I don't believe she left it alive."

Barbara Bullimore's brown eyes widened a little. She stared unblinkingly back at Lambert. There was an animation, even an excitement lighting up her plain face now. She could have denied it, made it difficult for them, made them bring a team to search the house, the garage, the car, in minute detail, scratching for the evidence of what she had done. She was too proud a woman to prolong the process with such deceit. Instead, she said in the low, even voice of one in a trance, "My brother is worth ten of that little tart! And she could have ruined him."

"So you killed her."

She rounded on him with flashing contempt. "I removed her from the world. So that Jason and other decent people like him could get on with their lives. People who could do some good in the world. I terminated her rottenness, that's all."

It sounded like an argument she had rehearsed often to herself, in the privacy of her bedroom, fighting the desperate loneliness which surrounds a murderer, who can confide in no one. Lambert said quietly, "I should have known you'd done that, much earlier. You said the first time we came here that you'd read that the girl had been strangled with some form of ligature. That never appeared in the press reports, because we didn't release it until the inquest. 'Strangled' is all that appeared in the press. But you told us about it, two days before it became public knowledge at the inquest."

She nodded, as if she, so proud of her own professional skills as a librarian, appreciated professional skills now in her adversary. "I checked the papers after you'd left on Saturday. But I didn't think anyone had spotted my little gaffe." She allowed herself a

184

rueful smile, as if she had conceded a vital pawn to an opponent who would make the most of it.

Lambert said gently, "You had better tell us what happened on that Friday night, Barbara."

It was the first time he had used her forename, an acknowledgement that it was over, an anticipation of the long years she would spend in confinement. The librarian Barbara would have bridled at such familiarity; the murderess merely nodded, as if she accepted it as a natural progression of events. "That girl said that Jason had been to bed with her, had enjoyed what she called 'his bit of fun' with her. I expect it was true. He's a bit weak that way – he means no harm, but he's a bit irresponsible at times. And women find him very attractive."

She shook her head, sadly but affectionately. Hook thought, Her brother is still about fourteen for her, a high-spirited lad who has to be protected. The trouble is, she doesn't want to let that young brother go, doesn't want to let him grow up. Aloud, he said, "And did Alison Watts say that she proposed to exploit Jason's weakness with her?"

"Oh, yes." She looked at the sergeant she had treated with cold hostility at their previous meetings with something like affection now. He seemed like a man who would surely understand what she had needed to do on that night. "The little hussy didn't want to talk to me about it at first, but I got it out of her soon enough. She said it was time for Jason to pay up for what he'd enjoyed. He'd – he'd had good service from her, she said, but it wouldn't do him any good if it came out at the school. There were times when she thought it might be her duty to write to the governors about it, she said, but she was sure that could be avoided, if we came up with a decent sum. Say about five hundred, to start with." Her revulsion for the moment and the girl flared out as she quoted the last phrases.

It was Hook, who seemed to have taken on the role of her confessor now, who had to prompt her. "And you told her you weren't going to be blackmailed like that."

"I told her what I've just told you. That my brother was worth ten of her and we weren't going to see his career ruined by a little slut like her."

"And how did she react to that?"

"She laughed in my face like the slut she was. Then she said we'd have to see what Jason had to say about that. I – I was a little worried by that. Jason is weak, in spite of all his talents. And he isn't as clear-sighted as me. He might even have been prepared to pay her something, in the hope of buying her off. But they always come back, don't they, blackmailers?"

"Almost always, yes."

"Well, I think it was at that moment that I realised something had to be done about Alison Watts." She smiled grimly, as if the thought of her action gave her satisfaction, even now, when retribution was at hand. It was one of the faults of obsessively tidy people that they saw decisive action as a way of putting things in order, even when it might be a wrong, morally impossible action. Barbara Bullimore saw herself as bringing order back into the lives of herself and Jason, ignoring the fact that she had turned the normal moral canons upside down to do so.

"So what did you do, Barbara?" Hook, who had never thought to use the familiarity of a forename with this Amazon of a female, urged her gently forward into the last phase of her awful story.

She leaned forward a little on the edge of her upright chair, as if taking these men into her confidence about some small, unimportant matter. "I said I'd see what money we had in the house. Then I went out into the garage and found a short length of the plastic-coated wire we use for tying up plants. It was just where I'd expected it to be." It would be, thought Hook grimly; there was no chance of this woman being rescued from herself by anything being in the wrong place. "When I came back in here, the girl had seated herself in that armchair." She indicated the chair by the empty fireplace with its high back towards the door. "I had never invited her to sit down, anywhere, least of all in Jason's chair." She added this detail triumphantly, as if it were the last item in the catalogue assembled to convince them of Alison Watts' worthlessness.

The pause told Hook that it was time again for some phrase from him to draw out the final section of what would become in due course a signed statement. "So that was the ligature you spoke of having killed her."

She nodded. "She had her back to me as I came through the door. She asked how much I'd managed to find in my piggy bank. She was only beginning to turn her head as I threw the wire round her neck." She smiled, an awful, childish smile, the smile which would, in due course, excite the psychiatrists called in by the defence. "It didn't take long to kill her. The wire was very effective, once I pulled it tight against her neck. But I saw the fear in her eyes, in her last seconds. It pleased me, that."

"But then you were left with a body."

"Yes. I closed her eyes after a minute or two. Decided I didn't like them staring out like that. They seemed to be following me round the room. Then I put her in the boot of my car and drove out into the Forest of Dean. I was waiting for it to get dark, but it seemed to take an awfully long time for that to happen. I didn't want to leave the car, somehow, even though the boot was locked. I remember I parked in the middle of the forest, near the Speech House, and read a book for quite a long time."

"And where did you put the body in the river?"

"Oh, I knew where I was going to do that. I was just waiting for it to get dark. I thought Symonds Yat might have people around, even at that time of night, so I kept well away from there. But I knew just where I wanted to park: a little bridge over the Wye near Goodrich. I only had about twenty yards to carry her down to the water, but when I got there, I decided to drop her off the bridge, to make sure she went in where the water was deepest. She was very light, really, when I got her over my shoulder. I put her down between the car and the river and tied the sack of coal I'd brought to weight her down onto her leg. I put the girl on the parapet of the bridge first, then lifted the coal and heaved it over the edge so that it took her down with it. They made quite a splash as they went. The water came right up and hit my face."

She seemed to find each detail more satisfying. Hook said, "And no one saw what you were doing?"

"No. It's a quiet enough spot. I'd have heard any vehicle coming when it was at least half a mile away, but not a single car came past in all the time I was there. It's only a minor road, with a nice old stone bridge. Jason and I have done a stretch of the Wye Valley walk from there. But I've not been back there since that night."

"Did you come straight home from there?"

"More or less. I sat in the car for about ten minutes after I'd got rid of the body, thinking about what would happen next."

"So what time did you get back here?"

"Just before eleven. I told Jason we'd been saying farewell to one of the library staff who was leaving, and went straight to bed."

"Did you tell him what you had done when Alison was posted as a missing person?"

"No, of course I didn't. I didn't want Jason involved in any way."

Love can be the most dangerous passion of all, when taken to excess, thought Lambert. It undermines reason and judgement faster than anything. He said, "Does he know now? Does he even suspect what you have done?"

"No, I know he doesn't. He's only a silly boy in some things, you know, despite his learning. An innocent at large."

It was a phrase which would haunt them in the weeks to come. They rode silently in to the station at Oldford, where she was put in a cell for the night. She turned back to Lambert and Hook as she entered the cell. "You'll let Jason know what's happened, won't you? Try to let him down lightly – it will be a shock to him. You – you'll tell him I did it for him, won't you? Tell him he'll need to look after himself in future."

The arms clasped across her formidable bosom and she reared herself to her full five feet ten as she watched them turn away. The broad, plain face lit up with a smile as the door was shut upon her.